Without warning, her eyes lost focus, and the room began to spin.

She grabbed a handful of curtain, but the dizziness robbed her of strength. Teetering, she began to fall and heard the material rip from the hooks. Muffled footfalls hit the carpet, followed by a man's strong expletive as he caught her above the waist—but he was off balance, and they both landed on the carpet.

Taryn rolled away and looked at her rescuer. Dan's green eyes glinted with amusement.

"You know, Miss Ross," he drawled, "we really have to stop meeting like this."

PAMELA GRIFFIN lives in Texas and divides her time among family, church activities, and writing. She fully gave her life to the Lord in 1988 after a rebellious young adulthood and owes the fact that she's still alive today to an all-loving and forgiving God and a mother who prayed that her wayward daughter would come "home." Pamela's main goal in writing Christian romance is to encourage others through entertaining stories that also heal the wounded spirit. Please visit Pamela at: http://users.waymark.net/words_of_honey

Books by Pamela Griffin

HEARTSONG PRESENTS

Don't miss out on any of our super romances. Write to us at the following address for information on our newest releases and club information.

Heartsong Presents Readers' Service
PO Box 719
Uhrichsville, OH 44683

Or visit www.heartsongpresents.com

Run Fast
My Love

Pamela Griffin

Heartsong Presents

Dedication and acknowledgments: Many thanks to all those wonderful people who helped me critique this book, and to those who gave of their valuable time by helping me with all the crime/legal issues and questions I had—especially to Larry Bullman, the Honorable Timothy Murphy, and public defender Anthony Odiorne—I give a special thank you.

As always, this book is dedicated to my Lord Jesus Christ, who, when I ran scared for a terrifying season, caught me in His loving embrace.

A note from the Author:
I love to hear from my readers! You may correspond with me by writing:

Pamela Griffin
Author Relations
PO Box 719
Uhrichsville, OH 44683

ISBN 1-59310-080-9

RUN FAST MY LOVE

Our mission is to publish and distribute inspirational products offering exceptional value and biblical encouragement to the masses.

All scripture quotations are taken from the King James Version of the Bible.

All of the characters and events in this book are fictitious. Any resemblance to actual persons, living or dead, or to actual events is purely coincidental.

PRINTED IN THE U.S.A.

Or check out our Web site at www.heartsongpresents.com

one

"Life is but a walking shadow, a poor player that struts and frets his hour upon the stage. . ."

And then is heard no more.

Taryn's mind whispered the last part of the Shakespearean quote. She felt more like a pawn in a deadly game than an actor playing a role. Though she wasn't that, either. Her panicked decision had brought her to this remote area, forced by fate's cruel hand. These past weeks were a checkerboard of black and white. Dark and light. Bad and good. Mostly bad. Very bad. It seemed an eternity that she'd sat, huddled in fear, on life's black square. Waiting. Hoping to be moved forward to the next patch of white—before the black swallowed her up and she disappeared forever.

Taryn's hands tightened around the fuzzy covering of the steering wheel as she forced her thoughts to the moment at hand. She pulled the car to a stop in front of a mountain lodge and cut the motor. Unpretentious and out of the way, the inn looked as though it would suit her needs perfectly. That is, if she decided to go through with her plan.

Ignoring her mounting anxiety, she took quick inventory of the place: the well maintained grounds and the snow-covered mountains that towered on all sides, encompassing the lodge in a secure little haven. The dark green wood building was pleasing to the eye and blended into the tall evergreens with an old-world charm, reminiscent of Vienna. High windows would afford a spectacular view of the mountains and neighboring ski lift to anyone inside. Icy-gray gingerbread trim outlined the gabled roof, giving the place a fairy-tale atmosphere, like something from *Hansel and Gretel*.

Taryn adjusted the rearview mirror and replaced an errant lock of auburn hair that had slipped from her chignon. Stalling, she picked up the local paper and scanned the classified ad for at least the tenth time that morning, as if by staring at the page she could summon courage from the tiny black print. She bit her long thumbnail, her gaze flicking back to the inn.

The other ad—the one in the outdated tourist's brochure at the gas station—had listed the lodge as "A great hideaway. An ideal place to escape your problems." Taryn wondered how many other strangers to the area took those words in a literal sense.

She fished in her handbag for the detestable horn-rimmed glasses that were part of her disguise and rammed them onto the bridge of her nose. With this accomplished, she fastened the top collar button of her brown dress at her throat, certain the stiff broadcloth would cut off her breath. If she didn't asphyxiate from nerves first.

Taryn opened the car door and stepped out, slamming it shut behind her. The noise echoed through the frosty mountain air like a series of gunshots. She jumped—almost lost her footing on the patch of slick pavement—and barely refrained from throwing herself to the ground for protection.

Cool it, Taryn. It wouldn't do for you to drop dead from a heart attack right outside Mr. Carr's cozy establishment. Or wind up with a sprained ankle and have them need to carry you inside.

She punched her fists deep inside her coat pockets and crunched along the pinecone-laden path leading to the lodge and up the three steps. Putting her hand to the cold metal handle of the door, she hesitated. She almost wished she knew how to pray, but she hadn't been inside a church since she was seven, when she visited the awe-inspiring silent building with her mother. Besides, surely God wouldn't condone what was about to take place. Yet what other choice did she have?

Squaring her shoulders, she swung the door open and moved into the foyer, stopping before the curved counter. Dark furniture with matching wainscoting and gold-flecked wallpaper gave the room an old-fashioned feel, as did the high brass chandelier that held lights in scalloped globes. Like something from a vintage movie. Taryn almost wouldn't have been surprised to see a young Claudette Colbert or Myrna Loy sashay into the lobby with bobbed hair, sequined dress, and a bright smile.

But she stood alone. Entirely alone. Gritting her teeth, she rang the bell for service.

An elderly woman hurried from a back room. Well, it wasn't Claudette or Myrna, but she could have blended in with that time period. Her blue-gray hair was cut and styled in a fashion reminiscent of the forties and meshed perfectly with the surroundings. Even her navy blue dress, with its ivory lace collar and brooch, seemed old-fashioned. Yet the effect was pleasant rather than eccentric.

The woman's kind blue eyes peered at Taryn from above a pair of silver-rimmed reading glasses. "May I help you, dear?"

"I'm Terri Ross. I've come for the job interview."

"Oh, yes, of course. Dan told me to expect you. I'm Veronica Carr. It's a pleasure to meet you, Terri." She gestured to a cozy-looking tapestry sofa in front of one of three tall windows that graced the room. Pine green curtains framed the magnificent view. "Please, do sit down and make yourself comfortable. My grandson conducts the interviews, but he's taking care of some business at the moment. I'm expecting him back any minute, though."

As if a stage manager had given a cue, once Taryn sat down on the sofa, a tall man clomped down the split staircase along the far wall. He approached the older woman, towering over her by a foot at least.

"It's worse than we thought, Gram," he said in a deep, rich voice. "We're going to have to replace the entire plumbing system. Markham says the pipes are corroded beyond repair."

"Oh dear. This isn't exactly an opportune time, is it?" Mrs. Carr plucked at the button near her waist.

"I'll call around for estimates. Markham offered us a good deal from what I can tell. Still, it would be wise to try to find something cheaper."

She patted his upper arm. "The Lord will find a way for us, Dan. He always does." She dropped her tone a few notches, though Taryn could still make out her words. "Miss Ross is here for the interview."

Daniel Carr turned and looked at Taryn for the first time. His eyes narrowing in speculation, he approached, his purposeful strides quickly eating up distance.

Taryn drew a deep breath. He certainly could hold his own against any roster of male movie stars in the business today. No question about it. His nose was a bit large, but the minor flaw did nothing to detract from his overall appearance.

Lean and bronzed, with muscles evident beneath a gray plaid flannel shirt and dark jeans, he reminded Taryn of a prowling wildcat. He seemed to possess a bottled-up sort of energy that unnerved her. His brownish-black hair grew long and untamed, swirls of it touching the base of his collar. A few locks lay along his forehead, and a five o'clock shadow covered his strong jaw, though it was mid-morning. But what riveted her most were his eyes. A clear, vibrant green, they pierced Taryn, mesmerized her. An electric shock seemed to zap her heart and rob her of the ability to inhale.

"Miss Ross, won't you come into my office." It wasn't a polite query but rather an abrupt command. After delivering it, he strode to a room beyond the counter, as if expecting her to follow.

Taryn blinked. Well, he may look as if he could play the

role of a dashing pirate, but he certainly didn't have any manners. Then again, neither did pirates.

She hid a wry smile and followed Captain Kidd into his cluttered office. At his curt instruction, she perched on the edge of a comfortable brown chair, feeling anything but at ease.

He took his place behind a desk. Settling his elbows on the chair arms, he steepled his fingertips together, propped his chin on his index fingers, and stared at her until she thought she would scream. A long-ago visit to the principal's office flashed across her mind, and like a truant child, she fidgeted. After about thirty seconds of his irritating perusal, Taryn decided she'd had enough. If this was how he treated prospective employees, it was no wonder management hadn't found someone to fill the position.

"Mr. Carr, I'd appreciate it if you wouldn't stare at me like that. It's unnerving."

"Ah, so you do have a voice." Dry humor laced the deep timbre of his words. He leaned forward, the chair giving a complaining squeak, and settled his hands on the desktop, clasping them. "I was beginning to think I imagined our earlier phone conversation. Sorry if I seemed rude," he said, not sounding sorry at all. "You're not exactly what I pictured. I was expecting someone more. . .mature. Your voice sounded huskier on the phone. Older."

"I'm over twenty-one and am used to a hard day's work, though I'm afraid I don't have any real job history." Taryn paused, hoping she wasn't sealing her fate with her words. "But that's because I spent the past seven years taking care of my father's household. I had no need to seek other employment at the time."

The pirate frowned. She wasn't going to get the position, she realized in panic, her heart sinking. But what else could she do? She was qualified for very little. Make that zilch.

Taryn offered a bright smile, hoping to elicit at least a

pleasant expression from his stony face and turn things around in her favor. He stared at her another few seconds then searched for something amid the paper mountains strewn across the desktop. Finding a ballpoint pen, he snatched it up and held it poised above a notepad. "May I have your father's number? For a reference?"

Taryn's smile faded. Unexpectedly, her eyes misted, and she groped for a tissue in her shoulder bag. "No—I'm sorry. He, um, died recently." She hoped he couldn't see how her hand shook. Locating a clean, crumpled wad, she retrieved it and brushed at her lashes, underneath the glasses.

His eyes grew softer, sympathetic even. "What about your mother?"

"She died when I was just a kid." Taryn sniffed, briefly averting her gaze to the back of the desk computer. "Look, I know it must seem odd for me to come here—a stranger to your town without any references or experience. Believe me, I understand your position. But I need this job."

His eyebrows lifted. She winced when she realized she was begging, but the funds in her wallet were low. And she couldn't withdraw anything from the instant teller machines, either.

They might find her.

"It won't be easy," he warned. "We're knee-deep in renovations now. Should I decide to hire you on, you won't have many housekeeping duties. You'll mainly be helping us with the restoration. At least for now. We hope to open again in two months, in time for Christmas—if we don't run into more problems. My grandmother and I have taken a lot of this on ourselves. Painting, wallpapering, some carpentry work—that sort of thing." He eyed her, his expression doubtful. "Sure you can handle something like that?"

"Yes," she replied without hesitation. "I have some experience doing odd jobs around the house that aren't related to housekeeping."

"Okay," he said with an easy smile. The change it brought to his face stunned Taryn. He looked more approachable, less daunting. The dimple that flashed in his cheek made him appear almost boyish. "To be honest, our former help took off with one of the guests last week, and you're the second girl who's applied for the job. The first girl we tried didn't know a mop from a sponge." He seemed suddenly to consider. "You do know the proper tools to use, I hope?"

Almost giddy with her small victory, Taryn gave an answering grin. "Yes, I do. You won't regret hiring me, Mr. Carr."

The smile disappeared, and his green eyes again seemed to bore twin holes into her skull. The lightning-quick change left Taryn more than a little anxious, not to mention the damage it did to her rapidly pounding heart.

"One important rule to consider, Miss Ross. We don't allow fraternization with the guests. None whatsoever."

She relaxed. "Believe me, I've no intention of socializing. I brought books to occupy my free time, and I like watching TV—alone. Mingling with the guests—with anyone for that matter—is the farthest thing from my mind."

Something about Dan Carr and the way he looked at her stalled Taryn's breath. She was accustomed to appreciative stares from men, but his probing, cold look made her uneasy. Could she get away with this if he was watching her all the time, as she was certain he would be? Worse, had he started to see beyond the disguise and recognize her, despite Taryn's painstaking measures to prevent such an occurrence?

"I'm glad we understand one another," he said. "All right, Miss Ross, we'll give it a shot."

Rising from his chair, he reached across the desk, one hand extended. Taryn stood and took hold of it. A tingle shot up her arm. His brow creased as he glanced at their clasped hands then just as quickly smoothed, and he gave her hand a firm shake.

"As I told you on the phone, starting pay is minimum wage plus room and board. After three months you'll be eligible for a raise. My grandmother will fill you in on the details and anything else I may have forgotten. You start tomorrow. I assume you brought your luggage with you?"

At her nod, he continued, "If you'll give me your car keys, I'll see to it."

"No, thanks." When he lifted his eyebrows, she quickly added, "I mean, I can handle it."

"Another rule—don't argue with the boss." His gaze roamed her figure. "You look wiped out. A sudden gust of wind might blow you clear down the mountain. Gram will take you to your room. Get some rest. You'll need it."

Grudgingly, Taryn handed him the keys. She was tired. Anyone forced to drive seven hours straight the previous day then sleep overnight in a dingy motel with paper-thin walls and noisy neighbors would be exhausted. But she'd had no choice.

She couldn't deal with the phantoms that haunted her life any longer. Neither the real invaders nor the imaginary fears.

two

Taryn returned to the reception area on shaky legs. She could scarcely believe she'd been hired. She only hoped the skills she learned while growing up under Mrs. Dreyer's tutelage would benefit her now. If it hadn't been for their housekeeper, Taryn would have been one lonely girl indeed.

She cast a glance up the stairs and frowned. Surely there couldn't be that much difference in the upkeep of a fifty-three-room villa and a cozy inn. At least she hoped not.

Mrs. Carr wasn't anywhere in sight, but a boy wearing a tan shirt with matching slacks sat atop a high wooden chair behind the counter. His athletic shoes tapped on the rail as he swiveled the seat around to face Taryn. Owlish eyes, huge and green, stared unblinking from behind thick glasses. He looked no more than six, but his impeccable appearance seemed out of place on one so young. His hair, the same dark coffee shade as her new employer's, lay combed into place, though it also had the tendency to curl. His clothes were crisply pressed.

"You looking for my great-grammy or my daddy?" He pushed the bridge of his glasses higher on his nose with one small forefinger.

So this answered the question of the little gentleman's parentage. Better for her that Dan Carr was married. Far better. She didn't need any further complications in her life.

Taryn smiled. "Your great-grammy, I think."

"She had to take care of a small 'mergency." He regarded her, his manner overtly serious. A carbon copy of his father.

"Oh? Nothing too terrible, I hope."

"Mr. Bowers hasn't got toilet paper." He lifted a hand to his mouth and snickered, for the first time looking and sounding like a real little boy. "I snitched it off the roll when Great-Grammy changed the towels in his room this morning."

Taryn fought to keep a straight face. "That really wasn't very nice, was it?"

The boy shrugged indifferently. "He yells at me a lot and says I'm always underfoot. But I'm not. I've never gotten under his shoes, though once I tied his shoelaces together when he was eating in the restaurant. I snuck under the table while he was reading his paper." He flashed her a wide grin, full of mischief. "He says I'm worse than Dennis the Menace. Who's Dennis the Menace?"

"You're kidding, right? Doesn't your daddy or mommy read the comics to you?"

He screwed up one side of his mouth in distaste. A dimple flashed in his cheek at the same place as Dan Carr's. Mentally Taryn shook herself, irritated with her wandering mind. She definitely didn't need to be thinking about Dan Carr again. Or his dimple.

"I like to read the nash'ul news," he answered with a professor-like air while he slid down from his seat. " 'Sides, Daddy's too busy and Great-Grammy doesn't read good anymore, even with her glasses. She says it makes her eyes hurt. And Mommy's dead. I gotta go eat my sandwich now." He made a beeline for a door at the rear of the room.

"Wait!" Taryn called after him before she could think twice. Sympathy for the boy warred with her shock at the unexpected revelation of Dan's marital status. She fished for something to say. "How come you're not in school? Is today a holiday?"

He tilted his head to one side and regarded her as if she wore a dunce cap. "I'm only five and three-fourths years old. I go to Kinder-Kind in the morning sometimes, but it's dumb. They only have books you color in and books for babies. I like big books, like Mark Twain's. Someday I wanna be Tom Sawyer. It's gotta be better than being me."

With that he turned, his rubber soles squeaking on the wooden floor, and took off at a trot down a hallway to the right.

"Paul—no running in the inn," Taryn heard Mrs. Carr order from somewhere beyond the papered wall. "You know better, young man. Take it outside."

"Yes, ma'am," his small voice piped back. But Taryn heard the light footsteps increase pace as Mrs. Carr turned the corner and walked into the lobby. The petite woman shook her head, a resigned look in her eyes.

"That boy! Sometimes I don't know what to do with him."

"He seems as if he could be a handful," Taryn agreed with a smile, thinking of poor Mr. Bowers.

"You don't know the half of it. Paul's gone through so much in his short life. I worry about him. It doesn't help that he's above the intelligence level of most children his age—genius level, I think, though we haven't had him tested. There are so many areas he's gifted in."

A troubled look flickered in Mrs. Carr's eyes, and she shook her head, as if by doing so she could push away her qualms. "But just listen to me—foisting our little family difficulties onto you, and on your first day here! Dan told me he hired you. I wouldn't want you running out the door."

The twinkle in her eyes led Taryn to believe the old woman was joking, but after meeting the young Paul Carr, she wasn't so sure. She would be certain to watch her back. And her bathroom supplies. At least her shoes had buckles and not laces.

"I think we're going to get along splendidly." The woman smiled up at Taryn. "The staff's rooms are at the back of the inn. I'll show you."

As they climbed the back stairs, Mrs. Carr filled Taryn in on the running of Pinecrest. "As Dan told you, we're behind since our last maid left us. Manuela was a bit of a spirited thing, always dating the local boys on her days off. It really shouldn't have come as such a surprise, finding her gone—" She stopped mid-stride and gripped the rail, her cheeks losing all color.

"Are you okay?" Alarmed, Taryn put a steadying hand to the woman's elbow.

Mrs. Carr took a few shaky breaths but managed a wobbly smile. "Mustn't overdo, and I believe I've done too much of that already. Not to worry. I'll go to bed extra early to make up for it."

"Are you sure you're all right?" Taryn hesitated, wondering if she should seek out Mr. Carr. "Why don't you go downstairs and rest? I can find my room if you'll give me directions."

The woman shook her head. "Just a few steps more and down two doors. I can make it."

Taryn followed, casting sideways glances at the woman. She felt terrible for having to put Mrs. Carr through this trouble. Yet the woman seemed determined.

Veronica stopped in front of a door, took a ring of keys from her pocket, and unlocked it, her hand still shaking. Taryn followed her inside to what was now home.

A loving touch had made the small room appealing. A colorful quilt with an intricate pattern was draped over the twin-sized mattress of an old-fashioned brass bed. Above that, hanging on the wall, a homemade sampler depicted a verse from the Bible—at least that's where Taryn assumed it came from since it showed a verse underneath. She'd never read a Bible so couldn't be sure. The message sent a shiver of apprehension tingling down her spine: "Lying lips are abomination to the Lord: but they that deal truly are his delight" (Proverbs 12:22).

Her eyes moved away from the accusing sampler, and she studied the rest of the room. A pine bureau with a rectangular mirror gave Taryn a view of herself from the waist up. Could that frazzled ghost looking back really be her? A wry smile pulled at her mouth at the memory of the person she used to be.

Mrs. Carr threw open a door leading to a small adjoining bathroom. Taryn promised herself a hot shower as soon as the woman left. Nodding toward the blanket, Taryn politely smiled. "Did you quilt that?"

"Yes, I did. In the days before arthritis struck."

"It's lovely. The whole room is."

"Thank you." Mrs. Carr's gaze went to the sampler on the wall. "My mother stitched that. I have one in every room, each with a different Bible verse or famous quote. She was a very talented soul."

"It's nice." Taryn squeezed the words from a tight throat.

"Isn't it? Well, dear, I'll leave you to get some rest. If you get hungry, go down before eight. The dining room stops serving then. It's the only part of the inn available to the public at this time. Come to my office in the morning and we'll go over the details," she said before closing the door behind her.

Glad to be alone, Taryn sank to the bed. She made a face at herself in the mirror and reached up to pull the tortoiseshell clip and bobby pins from her thick hair. The long mass of curls tumbled down over her back and shoulders in spirals. Her relief was enormous. She rubbed her fingers over her scalp, easing the tender flesh where the pins had stabbed. Pulling off the non-prescription glasses she'd found at a costume shop, she stared soulfully at her reflection.

Shadows flecked her eyes and dark circles ringed them. Her high cheekbones stood out more prominently than usual, due to the thinness of her face, she supposed. Her creamy skin had lost its rosy glow and looked pale, almost sickly. Frowning, she shook her head in disgust at the apparition. It was a wonder Mr. Carr had hired her, looking as she did.

A brisk knock at the door startled her. Taryn headed that way then hastily turned and retrieved the glasses from where she'd tossed them on the quilt. She jammed them onto her nose and opened the door a crack. Dan stood in the hall, a suitcase in each hand.

"Oh—my luggage." Taryn swung the door wide and stepped aside for him to enter. "Thanks. Just set it on that throw rug by the bed."

He stood rooted to the spot, gazing at her as if he'd never seen her, though thankfully without the recognition she dreaded. Uneasy, she shifted from one foot to the other while his probing eyes studied her face and hair. Her hair!

Seeming uncomfortable, he looked away from her and toward the flowered wall.

"Excuse me," she murmured. In a few steps she reached the bed and grabbed the tortoiseshell clip. Holding it in one hand, she attempted to sweep her unruly mane into a dignified do.

"No need for that."

At his abrupt words, her movements stilled. Astonished, she turned to where he stood in the doorway, still holding her bags.

"I'm sure it's more comfortable that way, rather than all stiff like you had it," he said gruffly. Clearing his throat, he stepped inside and set her two suitcases down near the foot of the bed. "That's some mighty nice luggage you have," he said loudly, in an obvious effort to change the subject.

Taryn glanced at the gold-monogrammed burgundy leather bags and shrugged. "A gift from my uncle."

"And that little white sports car outside. Is that also a gift from your uncle?" His words sounded suspicious.

"As a matter of fact, my car had engine trouble, and I did use my uncle's car." Uncle Matt had often told her if she needed anything, it was hers for the asking. And she had left a note behind, so he wouldn't contact the police, thinking his vehicle was stolen.

Taryn straightened to her full five-foot-ten inches. It did little good. Dan still towered over her.

"If there's a designated place for employee parking, just tell me where it is and I'll move the car. Otherwise I don't understand what the problem is." She wanted to say more but didn't trust herself to speak. It was becoming increasingly difficult to be civil to this irritating man!

This irritating man who was now her employer.

The mental reminder erased the frown from between her brows. It wouldn't do for her to lose this job within an hour of gaining it. Where else could she go but to yet another unfamiliar town to search for yet another unfamiliar job?

His hands went up, palms outward, as if to quell a rising argument. "Forget it. Sorry I said anything." He moved to the open door and hesitated. The glance he sent her way took her in from head to toe in a second. "Get some rest. You look like you could use it."

Once he left, Taryn let out a harsh breath. Working for that man certainly would test her fortitude. She had to be extra careful not to make any slipups. Remembering his vivid green gaze on her, she shivered. She'd felt like a bug under microscopic analysis. But his handshake earlier this afternoon had sent a hundred watts of electricity tingling down her spine.

Taryn firmed her jaw and set about unpacking. Dan Carr was much too attractive—and someone to avoid at all cost for her sanity.

૨૭

Insane. He must be.

Frowning, Dan paced the floor of the family sitting room. He stopped and stared out the floor-to-ceiling window on the west side. Snow-covered mountains clad with tall, dark evergreens stood outlined by the faint light of the moon, in a world of contrasting shadows and brilliance. The images were deceptive. Nothing seemed real.

"Daniel, what's wrong?"

Gram's soft voice broke the silence. He turned and studied her in her white pine rocking chair, a crocheted shawl around her small shoulders. She looked frail but still beautiful at seventy-six years of age. Her blue-veined hands lay folded over the cover of her worn Bible. She watched him, her eyes clouded with worry.

Covering the short distance between them, he hunkered down and took her thin fingers in his strong ones, managing a smile. "It's nothing, Gram. I'm just restless."

She straightened and fixed him with that all-knowing look. "Tell me another lie, Daniel William, if you dare. I know when you're hiding something."

Dan rose to his feet, releasing a forceful breath. He ran a hand through his unkempt hair. Whenever Gram used his first and middle names—and in that tone of voice—it was a lost cause to try and keep anything from her. She might be fragile on the outside, but she made up for any lack of physical strength with a strong disposition.

"Well?"

"I think I might have made a mistake in hiring Miss Ross," he admitted slowly, rubbing the tense cords at the back of his neck with one hand.

"Oh, Dan—no. She seems like such a nice young lady."

"Maybe. But some things just don't add up."

"Like what, for instance?" Gram clasped her hands on her lap and squared her shoulders as if readying for a debate.

"Like the fact that she owns some expensive things. Really nice things. But her clothes look like they came from the neighborhood thrift store. When I confronted her—just out of curiosity—she told me that her uncle gave her the luggage and loaned her his car."

"Well, then, there you have it." Gram looked pleased and perfectly willing to accept the information.

Dan shook his head. "Gram, you're a dear, but you're entirely too trusting."

"And you don't trust people enough, Daniel. Every young woman isn't Gwen. You can't judge them all by her standards."

Dan inhaled sharply, as if he'd been struck.

Gram flinched. "Hon, I'm sorry. That was a thoughtless remark on my part. You know I'd never do anything to cause you pain."

Dan nodded, though the sting remained.

Gram laid a gentle hand on his arm. "If you're suspicious of Miss Ross, why'd you hire her?"

"I let my feelings spur me into making the decision. Not a smart business move, I know. But she seemed so lost when she told me about her father. He's dead." Dan looked away toward the fire. He had almost wanted to put an arm around her in comfort when he'd seen the tears gloss her eyes. "And she so readily assured me that she could handle any task we gave her. She reminded me of an eager little kid, and I guess I folded."

Again, the memory of her vulnerable eyes—like sparkling silver coins behind those ugly horn-rimmed glasses—crossed his mind. He frowned. "But when I shook her hand I noticed it wasn't the hand of someone accustomed to hard work, the kind she told me she was used to doing. Her hand was soft, not a callous on it. And her nails were long. The polish wasn't even chipped."

Gram's mouth twitched. "I hardly think the fact that she has nicely manicured nails means she's a criminal waiting to pounce on us while we sleep, Dan."

He chose to let the amused remark slide. "Truth is, I don't believe she's done a real day's work in her life. That's when I first began to have doubts."

"Daniel, just what is it that you're saying?"

"I don't know. I just hope I haven't hired a thief. . .or

worse," he muttered, looking away from her steady eyes and into the flames jumping in the fireplace.

Gram studied his profile for a few quiet seconds. "I think you're letting your imagination get the best of you. Terri seems like a nice girl. I think she just needs some quiet time to help her recover from whatever's troubling her and some hard work to help her forget."

"Maybe." Impatient with Gram's habit of siding with the underdog, Dan shoved his hands in his pockets and returned to the picture window.

"She may not have one whit of experience, but she seems willing to learn, Daniel. And in this day and age that's hard to find. I feel we should just trust the Lord with this and ask Him to work it all out."

Dan exhaled softly, closing his eyes. Whenever Gram brought God into the picture, he knew he was sunk. "I hope you're right, Gram. I just hope you're right," he said under his breath, studying the thick line of trees that ensured the inn its privacy.

Time would tell. Yet that was little consolation if his theory proved correct and Terri Ross was on the wrong side of the law.

three

A sliver of sunlight spread across Taryn's face, pulling her from disturbing dreams. With eyes closed, she listened for the routine morning sounds of the household coming to life. First, Mrs. Baxter's orthopedic shoes would squeak up the stairs and down the hall as she brought her aunt a dietary tray of assorted melon balls and green tea. The sound of Cuddles's bell would follow, tinkling from the gemstone-studded collar around his neck as the Pomeranian trotted behind the maid. Dull clunks from the kitchen directly below would announce her uncle's Chinese cook preparing a king's breakfast for the rest of the household.

Taryn inhaled, expecting the earthy odor of autumn leaves to greet her from the open bedroom window. Instead she smelled pine and heard the sudden loud rumbling of a heavy-duty truck nearby.

Her eyes flew open. She blinked at the harsh, intrusive daylight and turned her head away. Small purple pansies on the wallpaper greeted her, not the elaborate gold swirls and roses she expected to see.

Confused, she shot to a sitting position and scanned the alien surroundings. The sampler caught her attention, and memories from the previous day swamped her. She scooted back against the brass rail while reality sank its teeth into her mind.

She was at Pinecrest, the newly hired employee of the Carrs. She was no longer in the San Fernando Valley, and she could never go back again. Not unless time reversed itself and eradicated the past. An event that wasn't likely to happen, no matter how she wished it.

With a heavy sigh, Taryn glanced at the green digital numbers on her portable alarm clock. Nine-thirty. *Nine-thirty?*

"Oh no!" She swung her feet over the edge of the mattress, struggling to banish the sheet that had wound itself around her legs. She must have forgotten to set her alarm or had slept through its beeps. She stripped off her flannel nightshirt, wishing for a reviving shower, but there wasn't time. After throwing on a pair of blue jeans and an ivory sweatshirt with "Get a Life" scrawled in blue across the front, she swept her hair up into its clip, slipped on her glasses, and bolted downstairs to the lobby.

Mrs. Carr sat at the reception desk, talking on the phone. Motioning Taryn to wait by holding one palm toward her, she finished conducting her business.

"Yes, that's right. We have four rooms that require immediate attention—there's water all over the bathroom floor. Three thirty? Can't you get someone here earlier than that? One of the rooms is occupied and. . .yes, yes, I understand. Well, please send someone as soon as you can. Thank you." Hanging up the phone, she looked at Taryn. "Good morning."

"Mrs. Carr, before you say another word I want to apologize for sleeping late. I promise it won't happen again."

The woman waved aside her concerns. "You must have needed it. Have you eaten?"

Yesterday after she'd awakened from a nap, Taryn had munched on a couple of granola bars and an orange stashed in her suitcase. Exhaustion and the need for solitude had kept her in her room the rest of the evening. She'd read a best-selling paperback to help idle away the time, but after the second chapter grew sleepy and retired early.

"I'm not much of a breakfast person. If I do wake up hungry, I usually have a muffin and a cappuccino," Taryn explained. "But I'm not feeling all that hungry this morning, so I think I'll pass."

"Stuff and nonsense," Mrs. Carr said in grandmotherly fashion. "You'll feel better if you eat a good meal before you start your day. Come along and I'll show you where the dining room is located."

Reluctant, Taryn followed the woman into a spacious, paneled room. Boston ferns in colorful planters hung from the ceiling at strategic points. Not one painting graced the wall—the view was enough to please any art lover. Tall picture windows afforded a fantastic scope of pine-covered mountains, with a ski lift in the background. Round tables were scattered around the room. Enticing smells of eggs, pancakes, bacon, and other delights wafted through the air, making Taryn's mouth water. Maybe she was hungry after all.

She followed Mrs. Carr into a spacious, well-equipped kitchen designed to prepare meals for large groups of people. Standing over the stove, a red-haired, buxom woman deftly flipped a row of pancakes with a spatula.

"Mary, this is the new maid, Terri. Will you please rustle her up something for breakfast?"

"Sure, and 'twould be a pleasure."

Taryn brightened. "You're Irish. My mother was Irish."

Mary smiled and began talking about her homeland, though she didn't waver from preparing Taryn's breakfast. Soon, a plate heaped high with eggs, bacon, pancakes, a muffin, and hash browns, along with a cup of coffee, was thrust into Taryn's hands.

Doubtful, she looked at the plate. "This is more than I eat in a day."

"A mite of food wouldn't be hurtin' you a bit. Me, I cannot seem to stop." Mary laughed and patted her ample belly. "Go on, enjoy yourself, and let me get on with my work." She shooed them out of her domain and turned back to the stove.

"Mary's a character, but she's a dear," Mrs. Carr said as they again entered the dining room. "She's been with us close to fourteen years now. She left Ireland after her husband passed away and their last child flew the nest. From what she told me, she came to visit their daughter, as well as to look up an old friend. Mary liked America so much that she decided to stay, and we've had the pleasure of her company ever since. Now sit and eat, while I fill you in on the goings-on of Pinecrest." Mrs. Carr motioned to a table in an alcove near one of the windows.

Seated in the cozy alcove, Taryn shook out her napkin and laid it over her lap. She stared at the bounty crowding her plate and wondered how she would ever get it all down.

"Staff has breakfast at six thirty, and we open the dining room to the public at seven. Likewise, lunch and dinner are served to the staff thirty minutes before we open to the public—at eleven thirty and six thirty. We've had to keep the restaurant open for business to help with costs, though we hope to open the lodge during Christmas break. That's our goal. Daniel already shared that with you, though, didn't he?"

Mouth full of eggs, Taryn nodded.

"At present there's one resident guest. He lives here year-round and has for some time. We don't normally do that, but he's a special case. Besides, he wouldn't leave when we closed the inn," she said with a twinkle in her eye. "And we couldn't very well kick him out on the stoop."

Taryn gave a slight grin, her mouth still full.

"Daniel told me that he went over what will be expected of you, so I won't repeat what was said," Mrs. Carr continued. "After we open, you'll assume the usual duties of a maid, and I'll go over your job list then."

Biting into a buttered apple cinnamon muffin, Taryn nodded again.

Mrs. Carr smiled. "Mary's a good cook, isn't she?"

Taryn finally managed to speak. "I haven't eaten food this good in quite a while."

"Mary has full authority in the kitchen. Cooking, cleaning,

meal planning. Her granddaughter Darlene sometimes comes to help out, too." Mrs. Carr put a finger to her chin. "Now, let's see, what else was there. . . Oh, yes. About your days off. Sundays and evenings after the dining room closes will be your free time. Daniel did warn you that you would be working long hours for a while, didn't he? We need all the help we can get to meet our deadline."

Taryn set down her juice glass. "I have no problem with working extra hours. I don't mind the hard work."

"Good! Today we're in a bit of a quandary. As you no doubt heard when I was on the phone, we're experiencing plumbing problems, and I'll need your help in moving our resident guest to another room. Unfortunately, his bathroom floor is one of those that flooded. Do you have any questions thus far, Terri?"

"Will I need a uniform?"

"Not until we reopen. What you're wearing is fine until then. Anything else?"

"Are you and your grandson the owners of Pinecrest?"

"Yes, dear. A legacy left to me by my late husband. I'm afraid neither Daniel nor I realized the expense of running such a place. My husband built Pinecrest when we were little more than newlyweds—much of it with his own two hands— and after all this time there are so many things that need to be replaced or renovated."

"It's a beautiful inn. Well worth the effort you're putting into it." Taryn nodded out the window, toward the ski lift. "Is that yours, too?"

"Oh, no. Pinecrest was here long before Bob Grady built his ski paradise. Our hope is that we can take the overflow from his lodge and provide transportation to the slopes. We've already negotiated a partnership of sorts, but with all the problems we've encountered just this week alone, we may have to wait until next year for such a venture."

A network of worry lines cobwebbed her forehead, and she stood. "I'll leave so you can finish your breakfast in peace. Mary will show you where the supplies are located—in the closet by the service elevator, next to the kitchen. Normally I would run you through the ropes, but today's just so hectic. . . ." She looked uncertain. "Do you think you can handle it, Terri, or would you prefer me to wait?"

"I don't think I'll have a problem as long as I know where everything is."

"Splendid. We'll go into all the nitty-gritty of it at a later date. For now, we'll put Mr. Bowers in room 214. Please prepare the room for him. Fresh linens are in the upstairs closet at the end of the hall." Mrs. Carr smiled. "I'm glad you've joined our little family here at Pinecrest, Terri. If you run into any problems or have any questions, you know where to find me." After giving Taryn's shoulder a reassuring pat, she headed for the lobby.

Taryn finished her breakfast, marveling that she'd eaten almost all of it. Already this peaceful mountain air was doing something for her. She gathered her dishes and returned to the kitchen. There was no sign of the Irish cook, so she rinsed off her things in the deep stainless steel sink and laid them on the counter.

Taryn left the restaurant—or dining room, as Mrs. Carr called it—and went in search of the service closet, certain she could find everything she needed without Mary's help. She ignored the rolling cart and grabbed a plastic carrying caddy from the high shelf, gathering what she thought she would need into it. Thankfully, the vacuum cleaner was a lightweight model and easy to carry, though it did have wheels. Armed with her arsenal of cleaning supplies, she took the service elevator and made her way to room 214.

Except for an incredible amount of dust, the room was in fairly good order. Taryn made quick work of changing the bed linens and left some fluffy white towels in the adjoining bathroom. Remembering little Paul Carr, she looked over her shoulder to the open door, making sure she wasn't being observed, and placed an extra roll of wrapped toilet paper on the high closet shelf. Surely Mr. Bowers would find it.

Next she unscrewed the cap to the furniture oil. She inhaled the bottle's clean lemon scent before taking a cloth and polishing everything wooden in sight until it glistened. The damask draperies were in need of deep cleaning, but there wasn't enough time for that, so Taryn fastened the appropriate attachment to the vacuum cleaner and did the best she could. Later, she would obtain Mrs. Carr's permission to take the curtains down from all the rooms and send them to the dry cleaner, as Mrs. Dreyer used to do.

After Taryn finished, she went downstairs, cleaning supplies in hand. Not seeing Mrs. Carr at the reception counter, she walked to the open door of the office where she'd been interviewed. The old woman sat behind the desk, riffling through the rat's nest of papers on top, obviously searching for something.

"Oh, where did he put that list?" she mumbled. "It's impossible to find anything on this desk!"

Taryn cleared her throat. "Excuse me. Sorry to bother you, but I wanted to let you know that room 214 is ready."

"Wonderful! I'll go and tell Mr. Bowers. He's been rather impatient about the whole thing. Crotchety old man," Mrs. Carr added with a chuckle.

Once she left, Taryn eyed the office, shocked to see how cluttered things really were. Nervousness had clouded her vision during the interview. How could anyone live like this?

Various-sized books and packets of papers in the built-in bookcase vied for space, crowding each other in haphazard confusion. One small circular window held a layer of film obstructing the view. The navy carpet was covered with stacks of unopened newspapers, magazines, and more books. An untidy mountain of receipts, ledgers, notebooks, papers, pencils, and who knew what else covered the desk. Over every piece of furniture lay a thin layer of dust, hiding the beauty of the dark wood.

Shaking her head, Taryn decided she would put this room to rights at once. She wondered how long it had been since Manuela vanished with her friend and left her employers in the lurch. Weeks? Months? Years?

Quickly she set to work. The minutes flew by as, under her busy hands, the room experienced a thorough makeover.

"Just what do you think you're doing?" a voice boomed behind her.

Startled, Taryn whirled around, lost her balance on the plastic crate on which she stood, and fell—into Dan Carr's arms. Her hands flew up to his hard chest, the fingers of one hand still clutched around the dust rag she'd been using with relish. Electricity shot through her, and her face felt as if it were blistering. She mumbled something incoherent, her tongue no longer seeming a part of her.

He held her a moment then forcefully set her from him.

"I asked you a question. What are you doing in here?" His voice was smooth, yet it held a dangerous undercurrent of anger.

Mortified by what had just taken place, Taryn felt her inherited Irish temper rise. "And just what does it look like I'm doing, Mr. Carr? Playing tiddledywinks? Surely you're intelligent enough to figure it out."

Dan's nostrils flared, his eyes sparking green fire. "Careful, Miss Ross," he said under his breath. "Didn't my grandmother tell you this room was off-limits?"

"Oh dear. I'm sorry, Daniel. I forgot." Mrs. Carr hurried into the room, bringing both their heads around. "I heard the commotion and came to see if anything was wrong." She lifted a brow, eyeing how close they stood. Taryn took a quick step backward.

"Dan, it's my fault," the old woman continued. "I forgot to tell her about your rule. Please don't blame her." She looked at the changed room. "But you must admit this is an improvement!"

Ignoring his grandmother, Dan studied Taryn, his eyes deadly serious. "In the future, Miss Ross, please remember this room is my private office, and I don't wish it disturbed. Is that understood?"

Taryn looked at the cluttered desk she hadn't yet had a chance to straighten and the overflowing wastebasket on the floor beside it. Her gaze then lifted to the sparkling window and the polished bookcase with its shelves of orderly books, thanks to her hard work.

"Yes, Mr. Carr, I understand," she replied, not understanding one bit. Just what was his problem? No matter, she would make it a priority to steer clear of him in the future.

❧

Dan stood at the circular window, grimly watching the men's progress as they worked to finish building the room that would house the spa and sauna. It had taken forever to convince Gram that if they wanted to compete with other lodges in the area, they needed this addition. Once they reopened and began to turn a profit, perhaps they could even hire a massage therapist. If they were able to reopen.

He stared at the crumpled bank statement in his hand. The situation kept getting worse instead of better. Their nest egg was long gone. The plumbing bill had drained much of what had been hoarded in the "home improvement account," and still the bills kept mounting. Gram wouldn't approve, but he might have to put a mortgage on the inn.

Moving away from the window, he scanned the office that once belonged to his grandfather. Memories ran rampant in his mind.

When Gramps was diagnosed with Parkinson's disease, Dan had been given power of attorney and made all business decisions—much to Gram's relieved approval. After Gramps died, Dan spent the next eight years wearing the new hat of manager and co-owner, stepping into his grandfather's shoes with confidence. His childhood was spent within these walls, observing his gentle grandfather's business acumen with childish eagerness and anticipation, learning the business, wanting to grow up to be just like Gramps.

But Dan had failed. Failed everyone he ever cared about. His desire for progress had been the start of Pinecrest's downfall. What would it do to Gram if he put a mortgage on the inn then couldn't make the payment in time? If she were to lose the home she loved, the home Gramps built for her. . .

No! He couldn't think along those lines. Since Gwen's death two years ago, Dan frequently questioned his decision-making capabilities. Long ago, he'd lost faith in his role as provider and protector. But if he wanted to come up with a viable solution, he would have to break out of this slump. What would Gramps have done?

Feeling a catch in his throat, Dan looked away from the ancient scarred desk. A framed and faded picture of his grandparents in their younger days caught his attention. Gramps proudly held up a sign he'd carved for the inn. Up until two years ago that sign had hung above the front door, welcoming guests to Pinecrest. A broken chain had relegated the sign to a seldom-used storage room, and Dan had forgotten to fix it, what with all the demands of everyday life. He would take care of that oversight soon—maybe even present the sign as a grand-reopening present for Gram. She was everything to him, she and his son. And this inn where Dan had been raised. Mortgaging Pinecrest would be like slicing one of his arteries and letting his lifeblood drain away. Yet what other choice did he have?

He ran an unsteady hand over his face. He supposed he should tell Gram of his decision, even though she was already ticked at him for the way he treated the new maid after finding her in his office. Seeing a woman in here, one besides Gram, had brought stabbing reminders of Gwen's deceit and reminded Dan of yet another of his biggest failures. His marriage.

Clenching his teeth, he tossed the crumpled wad onto his cluttered desk and watched as it bounced, rolled, and fell to the worn carpet on the other side. A dry chuckle escaped his mouth, even as moisture skimmed his eyes.

Okay, so maybe his office did look as if a pack rat had taken up residence. But it was *his* office and *his* mess. He didn't need anyone's unwanted interference. Especially if that "anyone" was a member of the opposite sex, with soft gray eyes hiding behind the ugliest pair of glasses he'd ever seen.

The sound of laughter—his son's and a woman's—brought his focus around to the open door. Curious, Dan followed the sporadic giggles to a front room.

Paul sat cross-legged on the floor next to an open cardboard carton. With clumsy fingers he wrapped an ivory figurine in a piece of newspaper splayed across his lap. The maid stood across the room and lifted a six-inch wooden carving of a bear, poised to attack, from the mantel. Light from the fireplace flickered over her tight hairdo, bringing gold flashes out of the dark red.

"So tell me, Paul," she said, her voice bright and more at ease than Dan had ever heard it. "Who told you that one?"

Paul shrugged. "Mr. Bowers. He may be mean, but he tells good jokes. Know what's black and white and blue all over?"

"No. What?"

"A penguin with a bad case of frostbite."

She groaned. "Now, that one was bad. Very, very bad."

The floor creaked as Dan took a step into the room. She

whirled around, her eyes startled behind the horn-rimmed glasses.

"Mr. Carr." A look somewhere between guilt and apprehension clouded her face. "We were putting these knick-knacks away for safekeeping. Your grandmother mentioned that men are coming to put in carpeting this Friday, and she wanted the knickknacks out of harm's way." She rubbed her palms down the sides of her jeans in a nervous gesture.

Dan turned his attention to his son. "School out already?"

"Yes." Paul stopped wrapping and looked up at him. "Can you stay and help us, Daddy?"

"Sorry. Not today. I've got an appointment with several cans of rose-colored paint that Gram wants."

"Can I come?"

"Not this time. I've got other errands to run besides. I'm too busy for games."

"Please, Daddy? I won't get in the way."

"No." When his son opened his mouth to protest, Dan put up his hand, cutting him off. "That's enough, Paul."

Sensing her disapproval, Dan shifted his gaze to the maid. Accusation shot from her eyes. Just where did she earn the right to judge him?

"I'd prefer it if you didn't pack the wooden figurines," he said, his words coming out clipped as he nodded to the bear she held. "My grandfather carved them, and they're very special to both my grandmother and myself. I'll box them up later."

Her mouth compressed in a straight line. She gave a curt nod and replaced the bear on the mantel.

Dan stared at her a moment longer, then spun on his heel and headed out the door. It had been a mistake to hire her. A big mistake. He'd wait for her to flub up before dismissing her, though. The last thing he needed was to rouse Gram's ire against him a second time. And Terri Ross was certain to make a mistake soon, of that Dan was sure.

❧

I never should've come to this place. Taryn slapped a sheet of newsprint over a brass angel and wrapped it briskly. The manner in which she'd seen that man treat his son reminded her of the way her father behaved toward her when she'd vied for his attention as a little girl. She hadn't possessed a big name or enough talent to garner her father's interest. And that was all that concerned Charles Rutherford.

Taryn knelt beside the cardboard box, her movements coming to a stop as she mulled over the past. After her mother died, the need for adult companionship—someone to love and care for her—consumed every waking moment, and Taryn tried hard to win her father's approval. Oh, how she had tried! Tap and ballet lessons. Voice teachers. At the tender age of fourteen, she'd even hired an acting coach. But it was never good enough for her father. She still held a mental picture of him shaking his head, disappointment clouding his eyes that he'd been cursed with a daughter who had no great talent.

Well, if you could see me now, Father, you would change your mind. Taryn lifted her chin in pained defiance, tears blurring her vision. *I'm giving the performance of my life—as good as any of the top stars in Hollywood!*

With a little more force than necessary, Taryn crammed the wrapped figurine into the last available space in the box.

"Are you mad at me, too?"

Taryn looked over her shoulder at Paul. Disappointment still fogged his eyes, but the tears Taryn had noticed when his father shouted at him had dried.

Couldn't Dan Carr see what his neglect was doing to his son? Did he even care? Taryn doubted it. The glimpses she'd had of men's characters didn't do much to build her faith in that gender. Her father had been absent more than present, and even when he did come home, he hadn't really been there. Uncle Matt, though he sometimes showed kindness, worshiped the god of money and put it above all else. The "manly" heroes of the screen whom she'd met were so full of themselves, a drop more adoration surely would have made them burst like overfilled water balloons. And then there was her bad-boy brother, Pat.

"Oh, Pat."

"My name's Paul," the little boy sitting across from her said crossly. "Not Pat."

Alarmed to realize that she'd spoken, Taryn stood and grabbed two more knickknacks from the mantel. "Of course it is, kiddo. I was just thinking aloud. And no, I'm not mad at you."

"Were you thinking about Pat?"

"Mm-hmm." Taryn became very intent on her work as she knelt on the floor and rolled the match to the other brass angel in a sheet of newspaper.

"Is she your friend?"

The question startled Taryn. She didn't bother to explain his error about Pat's gender; she was in hiding, after all, and the less known about her personal history, the better. But his innocent question stirred up the old desire again. The desire to have her playmate back and erase everything that had happened. Up until five years ago, Pat had been her best friend. As close as twins could get. And then had come the drinking, followed by the drugs—and who knew what else—that had turned him into a brooding, violent stranger.

Abruptly she looked away. "Pat was my friend. Once."

"You must still like her."

"Why do you say that?"

" 'Cause you're crying. People don't cry unless it's about people they care about. Like when my teacher Mrs. Forrester cried when Jimmy went to the hospital after his leg got broke on the playground. Or like Daddy cried when Mommy died.

He cried in his room for days. I heard him through my bedroom wall."

Taryn's movements stilled at this unexpected revelation. She didn't want to think of Dan as possessing anything but a heart of iron. For that matter, she didn't want to think of him at all. The idea that sensitivity might lurk beneath his gruff exterior unsettled her.

"Do you miss your mommy very much?" she asked softly, swiping one curled forefinger beneath her glasses. The boy was far too astute.

Paul gave one of his exaggerated shrugs. "I guess. Sometimes when she didn't have nothin' better to do, she'd read to me from one of her books. They had lots of big words I didn't understand and funny pictures. But she had a pretty voice, and I didn't mind—even if I didn't know what the stories were about. I'd sit with her in that chair over there." He pointed to a gold-colored velour chair in the corner. "She called me her own special little guide. A lot of the time she didn't want me around though. She had lots of headaches. Like me."

A pang twisted Taryn's heart at the emotionless words, which hid a wealth of emotion. She resisted the impulse to hug him, not sure how he'd receive it. "Tell you what, Paul. I was planning on going to my room during my lunch break and read a book, but I can do that anytime. I'd much rather sit here with you and read one of your books together. Your pick. Sound okay?"

His brow puckered in uncertainty.

"I'm not trying to take your mother's place," Taryn hastened to assure him. "That's her spot and always will be as far as I'm concerned. We can sit anywhere you'd like, or in any room you'd like."

"Can we sit outside? In the glider?"

Taryn blinked in surprise. Hardly any red showed in the

outside thermometer—the air had chilled and brought with it the scent of snow. "It's too cold for that." She was a California girl, after all, right down to her faded tan.

"I don't care." He crossed his arms stubbornly. "I want to sit outside. If you don't want to come you don't have to. But I'm going!"

His stalwart declaration reminded Taryn of herself when she was his age, shortly after her mother died. She'd been a terror to every nanny who crossed the threshold of her father's home, often pouting and using that stubborn stance to get her way. Now Taryn felt empathy for those long-ago dismissed nannies.

"Well, I suppose we could drink a cup of hot cocoa before going outside, and maybe we could wrap a blanket around us," she said.

"Great!" He shot to his feet. "I'll go and tell Mary to make some. And we'll read my new library book—*Moby Dick*. I'm gonna be a ship's captain someday, like Captain Ahab, and catch my very own whale!"

"I thought you were going to be Tom Sawyer."

"That was yesterday." He turned and sped from the room.

Taryn glanced at her wristwatch. She still had fifteen minutes before lunch, but how long would it take to make cocoa? If it were the instant variety, Paul would be back within minutes. But if Mary made it the old-fashioned way, and Taryn had a feeling she did, then she had time to pack the last box and tape all three of them shut.

She returned to the wrapping, her heart lighter. Though she'd told Dan Carr she wouldn't mingle with anyone on her free time, Taryn felt it was okay to spend time with Paul. Surely her employer's admonition did not include a little boy. Someone needed to be there for the child. And, strange as it may seem, Taryn wanted to be that someone.

❧

Dan slammed the door of his truck, his display of anger lost in the sharp staccato bangs from pounding hammers and other construction going on around the outside of the inn. It had not been a good day.

First, the machine that mixed the paint wasn't working right at the hardware store, and the newly hired teenager had gone in search of his boss. When the pimple-faced boy came back a full ten minutes later with the obvious report that the machine was broken, Dan gritted his teeth and asked when it would be fixed. To his frustration, the boy shrugged and said, "I'll go ask." He ran off before Dan could stop him, but this time Dan didn't wait for his sluggish return. He'd stormed out of the store—and accidentally knocked into a stout, middle-aged tourist, who dropped her purse in shock. Apologizing for his clumsiness, he stooped to the sidewalk and picked up the numerous items that had toppled from her ridiculously large handbag, while she watched in a huff and complained about the rudeness of the locals. Afterward, he headed to the bank. Another mistake.

Mr. Fredericks had taken the week off due to a death in the family. Any sympathy Dan normally would have felt for the man was lost; the fate of the inn crowded all else from his mind. When the receptionist offered a substitute, Dan declined. Lyle Fredericks was an old friend of his grandfather's and understood the situation, whereas a stranger might not.

To top it all off, on his way home, after taking a sharp turn on the road, his truck had a blowout and he'd had to put on the spare tire. Now he'd need to purchase another one—as if he didn't have enough money problems already. What else could go wrong?

Thrusting his greasy hands deep into the pockets of his coat, he rounded the front corner of the inn. The picture of the new maid nestled in a blanket next to his son stopped him in his tracks. Each of them held one side of a large book, their heads bowed in concentration over the pages, while she put the glider in slow motion with her brown loafer. The scene tugged something deep in his heart, pulled at his defenses—and was altogether too disturbing.

Dan crunched across the snowy path, his gait rapid. "Miss Ross?" His voice came out as sharp as the icicles lining the eaves.

Her head snapped up, and she slowly closed the book, expression wary. "Yes, sir?"

"You were told that we are on a tight schedule to get the inn opened by Christmas. I don't recall you frittering away your time with my son as being on the list of your daily activities."

She shoved the book at Paul and stood, sending the glider into a crazy dance. "So you're saying I no longer get a lunch break?"

"Lunch break?" Dan repeated stupidly. He glanced at his watch. The black digital numbers confirmed her statement. Heat seared his face at the oversight. "Er, of course you get a lunch break. You have six minutes until you report back to work."

"Thank you so much for the reminder." Her words were laced with vinegar. She turned to the boy, her face softening. "I enjoyed our time together. You're a very good reader."

"Can we do it again sometime?" Eagerness filled Paul's voice.

Her gaze lifted to Dan's, silently challenging him. "I'll leave that up to your father. I'm just an employee here, after all. And work at the inn takes precedence over everything else. Isn't that right, Mr. Carr?"

Dan's jaw hardened. "Paul, go inside, and take the blanket with you." His words were low and even, his steady gaze never leaving hers.

A hint of alarm widened her gray eyes, and Dan felt smug. Good. Let her worry about her job for a minute. She was much too outspoken and didn't act anything like a maid should.

After the door closed behind Paul, Dan crossed his arms and glared at her. "Miss Ross, let's get something straight right from the start. When it comes to my son, your opinion doesn't count, and your interference isn't wanted. Is that understood?"

"Yes, sir." The words were bitten out.

Adrenalin rushing through him, he uncrossed his arms and took a few steps in her direction. "And I don't appreciate you making me look like the bad guy, either!"

"I wasn't—"

"You were."

"If anyone was making anyone look like the bad guy—it wasn't me."

"And what is that garbled logic supposed to mean?"

"It means that your son needs a father, but like most fathers, you're too busy to care." Her words flew at him, slashing him deeply with their blades of truth. "If you could've seen how upset he was when you told him he couldn't go with you. . ."

Dan had seen the tears of disappointment in Paul's eyes, but for this woman to point it out to him was too much. "Miss Ross, if you want to keep your job at Pinecrest, you'd better keep that little turned-up nose of yours out of my affairs. And that includes my son's. And my grandmother's," he added for good measure. "This is your first and final warning."

Her face went strangely blank. She seemed to deflate before him as the fire sputtered from her eyes, like a flame snuffed out in a breeze. "Yes, sir," she said in a wisp of a voice. "May I go now?"

Upset that he'd lost his temper, but even more upset that he should care that he'd hurt her, Dan gave a curt nod and focused his attention on some nearby trees. He heard her light steps scurry across the wooden porch, followed by the door opening and clicking softly into place.

Frustrated, he kicked a pinecone, then watched it sail twenty feet through the air, land, and make a soft dent in the shallow snow. Just who was Terri Ross? Why had she come to Pinecrest? And why did he feel as if he'd just trampled an injured bird?

Dan stared back at the inn. He had a mile-long mental checklist of questions regarding the new maid—and a bad feeling that he wasn't going to like any of the answers.

four

"Terri, over here!"

Taryn hesitated. Her gaze flicked to the table where Veronica sat. Dan Carr had warned her to stay away from his family. Yet at the same time she couldn't be rude.

"Please join me." The older woman motioned toward the opposite seat when Taryn approached the table. "I hate to eat alone."

"Where's Paul?" Taryn set her plate and glass down and slid into a chair.

"He has a tummy ache. Nothing serious. He often has these little stomach upsets."

"Oh, I'm sorry to hear that. He seemed fine when we read together earlier."

"I'm glad you brought that up. He told me about this afternoon."

Taryn went rigid, wondering if she would receive two tongue-lashings within a twenty-four-hour period. Mrs. Carr reached across the table and patted her hand.

"Relax. I heartily approve. I haven't seen Paul this excited in a long time. He's been talking nonstop about reading with you and can't wait to do it again."

"I enjoyed it, too. He's extremely smart for a boy his age and way above his reading level." Taryn relaxed her grip on the napkin in her lap and took a sip of water, deciding not to mention Dan's ultimatum. No use upsetting the woman.

"The kindergarten he attends offers no challenge for him. He gets bored easily. There's a private school I've heard about for gifted children, but we just can't go that route right now.

Which brings me to one of the reasons I asked you to sit with me. There's something I wish to discuss with you."

Mrs. Carr leaned forward, her gaze intent. "I've given it some thought, and I'd like you to continue spending time with my great-grandson when you can, if that's agreeable to you, of course. Daniel is too busy with the inn to give the boy enough attention, and I. . ." She sat back, her face crumpling. "Well, I'm too old to be the companion Paul needs. Unfortunately, there are no children in the area for him to play with, either."

"Mrs. Carr. . ." Taryn bit the inside of her lip, mentally forming her words. "It's not that I wouldn't love to spend time with Paul, but have you talked to your grandson about this?"

"Talked to Daniel? Why, no, but I should think he would approve. From what Paul shared with me of your time together, you strike me as having a way with children. And please, Terri, call me Veronica." Her eyes brightened as she lifted her gaze and looked beyond Taryn. "Why, here comes Daniel now."

Taryn almost choked on her rice. Grabbing her napkin, she pressed it against her lips. She took a sip of water, sensing his presence behind her before she saw him. Lifting wary eyes, Taryn met his solemn gaze as he came into view and turned his head to look at her. None of the hardness or anger that etched lines in his face earlier was apparent. But neither was there any welcome.

"Daniel, don't just stand there," Veronica said, sliding over to make room for him. "Sit down, join us. I've something I wish to discuss with you." She frowned. "Aren't you eating?"

"I ate earlier. Where's Paul?" He sank into a chair, a tall mug of coffee in his hand. His long legs accidentally brushed Taryn's, startling her.

She pulled her knees back as far as possible in the small space between the seats, hoping to avoid further contact. His mouth twitched. Now he was laughing at her? Her ire kindled, she lifted her chin and stared him down. His eyes narrowed, and he averted his gaze to his grandmother.

"Paul had another little stomach upset. He'll be fine." Veronica cut a short sliver from her baked chicken breast. "Terri and I have been talking. About Paul, as a matter of fact." She brought the fork to her mouth.

"Oh?" The word came out soft, but the razor sharp stare he swung on Taryn effectively sliced her prideful anger to smithereens. "What about Paul?"

"Well," Veronica began, "Terri spent a half hour with him today, and quite frankly, I haven't seen Paul this happy or excited about anything in months. I suggested she spend more time with him on a regular basis."

"Re—ally?" The word was drawn out, accusing.

Taryn stared at her untouched chicken filet.

"Yes. She seems to have a wonderful affinity for him. I do believe she's a godsend." Veronica sent a smile her way.

Taryn fidgeted, wishing she could melt into the chair and disappear. From across the table Veronica's face beamed at her with gratitude while Dan glowered at her, leaving little question as to what he thought.

Taryn cleared her throat. "Maybe it isn't such a good idea, Mrs. Carr, what with all that needs to be done around the inn—"

"Veronica. Call me Veronica. And Paul is much more important than any work needing done, as I'm sure Daniel would agree. Besides, it wouldn't be for more than an hour a day. There'll be plenty of time left over, and it shouldn't interfere with your other duties."

"Don't you mean a half hour? That's what I get for lunch."

Veronica looked appalled. "Why, Terri, I wouldn't expect you to sacrifice your lunch break! This would be separate. Isn't that right, Daniel?"

He continued to stare at Taryn while addressing his grandmother. "Whatever you think is best, Gram. I need to get back to work." He picked up his mug and stood. "Miss Ross, after you've eaten, I'd like a word with you in my office."

Taryn nodded. She tried to swallow the lump that had risen to her throat by taking a sip of water. After Dan left, she pushed her plate away. The thought of pushing food down her tight throat soured her stomach.

"Don't let him get to you, dear," Veronica soothed. "To quote an old cliché, his bark is much worse than his bite. He's had a lot on his mind lately concerning the inn. Why, on a good day, Daniel can be quite charming."

Charming? Dan Carr? The ludicrous thought almost made Taryn laugh. But the angry disgust that had simmered in his eyes with the final glance he'd directed her way doused any feelings of amusement. Taryn could see her dismissal close at hand. And this time she doubted Veronica would be able to prevent it.

๑

Dan jammed his fingers into the back pockets of his jeans and stared out the office window. Twilight cloaked the steep mountains with shadowy purple, giving the surroundings an eerie cast, like something out of a Grimm's fairy tale.

His mind went to the conversation he'd just left, and he pressed his lips into a thin line. Trust Gram to take that girl under her wing, especially after the doubts he'd raised on the maid's first night there. Like an aged Pollyanna, Gram moved through life determined to find the good in everyone. Dan doubted any young woman in today's world possessed such redeeming qualities as unselfishness or goodness, but he knew Gram would do her best to prove him wrong. And she'd use Terri to do it.

Well, he wouldn't be played for a fool this time. He knew the truth; he'd had more than enough experience. It was a dark blotch in his timeline that he was still trying to rub out. Yet the pain always remained, and the blotch wouldn't go away.

No sound alerted him, but Dan sensed the maid's presence. Slowly he turned and studied her where she stood in the doorway. He nodded to the chair facing his desk. "Sit."

With jerky movements, she did as he told her. Dan could see apprehension mount in her eyes, though they gazed back at him steadily. Her helmetlike bun still lay molded to her head, but through the course of the day several strands had escaped near her temples to spiral down her shoulders, softening the slightly angular line of her jaw. She clasped her hands in her lap and straightened her back, as though preparing for a firing squad.

The thought made him uncomfortable. He didn't want to feel anything for her except maybe indifference. He especially didn't want to feel sympathy or concern. But he didn't want her to think he was some kind of ogre, either.

"Relax." He cleared a stack of nature magazines from the edge of his desk and dropped them to the carpet. She gave a startled little jump at the loud *smack* they made. Her gaze dropped to the magazines and then went to her lap.

Frowning, Dan leaned against the cleared space and crossed his arms over his chest. "I haven't called you in here to fire you, Miss Ross. So you can stop trying to look like a pitiful little martyr waiting for me to burn you alive at the stake."

Her eyes snapped to his. Good. At least her spirit was back. He'd much rather deal with a spitting lioness than a helpless kitten.

"I wanted to clarify some things," he went on. "First and foremost, my grandmother and her wishes are important to me. She's the only mother I've known, and I wouldn't hurt her feelings for the world. It's obvious she's taken with you. It's equally obvious that you've done something to ingratiate yourself with her. I'm not happy about it, but the damage is done, so that's that. Where she got the crazy idea that it would do Paul any good to spend time in your company is anybody's guess. But if that's what she wants, I'm not going to refuse her. Unless you foul up, of course."

She lifted her chin. "Your flattering words and high vote of confidence are extremely encouraging, Mr. Carr. Thank you." Her gaze spit molten silver at him, though her voice remained level.

Unbidden, a small smile twitched his lips. He rubbed his bristly jaw with his fingers to cover the slip. Her feistiness both annoyed and amused him—but it was definitely preferable to the silent, scared waif that had entered his office a few moments ago. Still, it was high time she learned who was the employer and who was the employee.

"I've made no bones about my feelings concerning your interference in our lives, Miss Ross. To state otherwise would be a lie. You were hired on to help us with the inn, not to be a baby-sitter or a counselor. But for Gram's sake, I'm willing to give this experiment with Paul a trial run, as long as it doesn't interfere with your work. The work I hired you to do."

"Contrary to your belief, Mr. Carr, this wasn't my idea. And, just for the record"—she sat up straighter—"I didn't finagle my way into anybody's good graces. I like your grandmother. I'd never manipulate such a sweet old lady."

Sincerity shone from her eyes, disturbing him. Gwen had often affected such a look, and the reminder punctured his heart with doubt.

"Meaning you'd manipulate one not so sweet?" His voice was ominously low. "Or not so old?"

"That's not what I meant, and I think you know it."

"Never mind." Weary of the entire conversation, Dan waved his hand to cut off her words. Maybe he preferred the quiet, meek kitten after all. "I didn't call you in here for an argument. I just wanted you to understand how things stand between us."

"Oh yes, Mr. Carr, believe me, I do understand." Tears glistened in her eyes as her chin elevated another notch. "You've made it abundantly clear. You don't approve of me, and you don't like me. But let me tell you something that may shock you. Your views don't matter. I know who I am and what I'm capable of achieving, and your low opinion of me won't keep me from doing the best job I can!"

"And just who are you?"

She blinked. "What?"

"You said you know who you are. I'm curious to know just who that is. The fact is, I know very little about you, Terri Ross."

"I—" She nervously twirled a gold ring on her right hand. "I'm nobody special. What I meant is that you can trust me with your son. I'd never do anything to hurt Paul. Or anyone else for that matter."

He stared at her long and hard, wishing he could unearth her secrets, for she was obviously hiding some. Anxiety clouded the light gray eyes behind the glasses, and her throat rippled as she swallowed hard.

"You may go, Miss Ross. But be warned—I'm watching you. One mistake, and you're out the door. And if you ever say or do anything—and I mean anything—to hurt my family, you'll wish you'd never stepped foot onto Pinecrest."

Her gaze grew troubled, almost fearful, making him wish he hadn't added that last bit. Did she think he'd resort to physical violence? Dan would never lay a hand on a woman in anger, but now he realized his words could have been misconstrued. Before he could clarify, she jumped to her feet and hurried from the room.

❧

Taryn paced the worn carpet, arms wrapped around her waist. Over and over, Dan's parting threat echoed, a ruthless chant in her mind. Oh, why couldn't she learn to hold her tongue? Why did she flare up and explode like a Roman candle whenever she was in his company?

All her life she'd never watched her words, never been trained to, never needed to. After twenty-three years of speaking her mind, the concept of changing her ways seemed inconceivable. Yet if she wanted to avoid trouble—namely Daniel Carr—she'd better give it a better than decent try. She had no doubt that Dan would contact the police if she hurt his family—which she would never do. Yet Dan was wont to jump to conclusions concerning her. Suppose he wrongly accused her and then called the authorities. When they ran a check on her they would realize there was no such person as Terri Ross. What then?

She had to get out of here.

Grabbing her wallet off the dresser, Taryn looked inside it. Four dollars and seventy-three cents. Hardly enough to buy gas to get out of town, much less acquire a decent meal, and she detested the thought of sleeping in her uncle's car, as she'd done twice. No, she had no choice but to stay at Pinecrest—at least until she received her first paycheck.

Her fingers went to the gold chain tucked underneath her flannel sleep shirt and satin robe. The robe she'd brought from home; the shirt she'd bought at a used-clothing shack off the road. In her crazed three-minute packing job she'd forgotten to pack a lot of necessary items and needed to buy them after her escape. She pulled out the smooth heart-shaped locket and slid it back and forth on its chain while she paced the room. Both the ring, which now barely fit her pinky, and the heart-shaped charm were long-ago presents from her mother for her seventh birthday.

Bang!

A gunshot shattered the night. Taryn whipped her head around in the direction of the noise. She stood, petrified, then ran to the window and snatched aside the drape. She couldn't see a thing. Only dark, sinister-looking trees. Anyone could be hiding within their recesses—anyone.

Bang! Another shot exploded outside.

Terrified, she ran. The pocket of her robe caught on the knob as she escaped out the door. In her panic she didn't stop to unhook it, but frantically pulled the ivory material. The seam ripped, and she was free. She fled down the stairs to the lobby, her rapid breaths coming in gasps.

All logical thought fled.

The nightmare had become reality.

five

Hunched over his desk, Dan estimated the amount he would need to pay McClean's Carpets. He hated to see the wooden floor covered, but it was so deeply dented and scarred after more than fifty years of use they'd had little choice. A short shag carpet was cheaper than refurbishing the floor, especially with the going-out-of-business sale McClean's was currently holding.

Heaving a sigh, Dan settled back in his chair and rubbed the back of his neck. Another *bang* shattered the peace outside, and his gaze went to the round window.

Immediately he heard footfalls clomp down the stairs in the lobby, followed by the sound of rapid shuffles—as if the person running wore slippers.

Had Paul had another nightmare? Dan rocketed to his feet, his wheeled chair shooting backward and slamming against the bookcase. He wrenched open the door and stepped into the darkened lobby.

The maid sped around the corner, the hem of her robe flapping against her bare legs. She stopped, as if uncertain, and then ran toward him. The muted yellow lamplight from his office made her appear ghostly. Her face was blanched, and the pupils of her eyes had dilated, darkening the gray irises to black. Her glasses were missing.

The shock Dan received at seeing Terri there, and at this time of night, tripled when she threw her arms around his shoulders. She clutched the back of his flannel shirt in a death grip.

Automatically he put his arms around her to steady them

both. Dan blinked in confusion. She burrowed her face against his chest, trembling like a child awakened by a severe thunderstorm. Feeling awkward, Dan patted her back. Her hold tightened, and she sniffled. Now she was crying?

The desire to protect surged through Dan like an uncapped geyser, stunning him with its intensity. "It's all right," he said close to her ear. "Did you have a nightmare?"

She shook her head against him. "Gunshot," she whispered. Dan could barely make out the muffled word.

"Gunshot? Oh. That wasn't a gunshot. It was backfire from a neighbor's car."

At first, Dan didn't think she'd heard him. But then the trembling lessened and her gasps slowed. "It was a. . .car, not a gun?"

"Not a gun."

Her breath warmed his shirt where she'd dampened it with her tears. She felt so soft and comfortable in his arms, and her sweet vanilla scent encouraged him to gather her even closer. If he lowered his chin just a little, it would rest on top of her curly hair. She fit against him as if she were made to be there. . . .

Realizing his thoughts were taking him places he had no business going—or even wanted to visit—he grasped her wrists and firmly but gently broke her hold. She looked up at him in pained confusion. Dan could tell the moment realization hit. Her eyes enlarged even more and her face instantly regained all its color. She jerked away from his grasp.

"I'm sorry. It was the shot. . .and then thinking. . .I mean, I wasn't thinking—clearly, that is. . ." She took a step in retreat, her slender fingers pulling the ends of her already tight sash.

"It's okay. No harm done."

She gave a short nod. "When I heard the bang I thought someone was hurt or. . .or something."

"It was just backfire from Jim Perrow's old Chevy," Dan reassured, noticing how large her eyes were without the horn-rimmed glasses. And the light gray irises were fringed with dark brown lashes—almost black. Unusual on a red-head, but nice. Very nice. He noticed something else he'd never seen. A thin white scar curved from her temple along the top edge of her cheekbone and below the outside corner of her eye. The glasses had helped to hide it before.

"It happens a lot," Dan said as an afterthought. "His car backfiring, I mean."

She cleared her throat, her gaze dropping to the floor between them. "I should go back to my room now. Thanks for. . .well, just thanks."

"No problem."

She started to turn away.

To his shock, unexpected words rushed from his mouth. "You still look a little shaken up. Gram has some herb tea that she swears by. She says it helps her relax. I thought I might give some a try. I need a break from doing the bills. Want to join me?"

Surprise flickered in her eyes, followed by wary resignation. "No. But thanks for asking."

"You sure?"

She nodded. "I overreacted. I feel silly enough as it is. Besides, the carpet people are coming early in the morning, and I should get some sleep. There are still things your grand-mother wants done in that room before the workers start." She glanced away. "Well, good night."

"Good night." Not sure what exactly had just happened between them, or why he should feel such a stab of disap-pointment that she'd declined his company, Dan watched her walk away until she turned the corner and disappeared from sight.

❧

Backfire from a car! How humiliating.

Taryn stuck her hand into the pocket of her robe, only to

have her fingers slide down the torn material. Remembering the damage she'd done to her garment during her mad dash out the door, she studied the ripped pocket on the right side and the gaping hole at the seam. Terrific. This had been one of the few articles of clothing she'd brought that was truly hers—not secondhand. Now she'd need to buy another robe since she didn't know how to thread a needle, much less sew. Hopefully there was a thrift store nearby where she could pick one up for a couple of bucks. Boutiques and shops like the ones on Rodeo Drive were no longer an option.

She shut the bedroom door firmly behind her. That cup of tea had sounded so tempting, though she couldn't picture someone like Dan Carr drinking herbal tea. Black, bitter coffee seemed more his speed. Mortification had forced her to leave his company, and Taryn again felt her face warm. She couldn't believe she'd done something as idiotic as to catapult herself into his arms.

When she'd rounded the corner and had seen Dan standing there—so tall and strong and secure—she hadn't thought clearly in her panic. The sight of another human being to share the horror had drawn her to him, as had the relief that swept through Taryn when she saw that he hadn't been shot. Even if they didn't get along well, she certainly didn't want to see him injured or dead. She would have reacted with the same relieved fervor had it been anyone else who exited the office at that precise moment. Grizzly Adams, for instance. Or the Hunchback of Notre Dame.

The ridiculous thought almost made her smile. She had watched too many movies since she'd been on the run. The escape into fictitious lives and lands had been a temporary respite. The shadowy future was always there, its door slowly swinging open and forcing her to look into the darkness beyond. Mentally she backed away from that door, wanting to stay in the well-lit corridor of the present—her present—the present she'd shaped for herself upon coming to Pinecrest. The actual present wasn't an option. It could only destroy her and everyone else she loved.

She supposed, in a way, she'd created her own fictitious world, like those run-away-from-reality plots in the movies. And though such a pretense was preferable compared to her life as Taryn Rutherford, the playacting didn't deal with the fear that gnawed at her daily—the fear of being found out. Soon the director would yell "Cut!" and she'd be forced off the Pinecrest set, to face her nightmare all over again.

Taryn shivered and hurried to bed. She pulled down the thick quilt and slid between the sheets, robe and all. Unwanted, the feel of Dan's muscular arms around her came to mind. She squeezed her eyes shut and tried to picture white fleece on four-legged creatures jumping over a low fence. Instead, she relived the feel of Dan's reassuring embrace.

Taryn flopped over onto her stomach and clutched the pillow, burrowing her face into it. But the memory refused to dissolve. And for a fleeting moment she wondered what her life might have been like had she met Dan Carr under different circumstances.

&

"Hey there!" Taryn greeted as she walked into the kitchen.

Paul sat on a high stool he'd pulled up to the wooden island in the center of the room. Chocolate chip cookies and a glass of milk sat in front of him. Mary stood on the other side of the island, rolling out dough for one of her delicious goodies.

Mary offered Taryn a bright smile. "Hungry? I made some extra sandwiches."

"Yes, as a matter of fact, I am. I spent all morning moving things upstairs to the storage room—well, what I could—before the men from the carpet place arrived." She slid a stool beside Paul's and sank onto it.

He looked up from his cookie, his upper lip sprinkled with

crumbs and wearing a milk mustache. "The carpet men are here? Can I watch them put the carpet down?"

Taryn thanked Mary for the chicken salad sandwich she set before her. Stalling, she lifted one of the triangles off its large lettuce leaf and took a bite, savoring the sweet red grapes inside. Veronica had made it clear that she didn't want her grandson in the vicinity while the men worked, so Taryn considered the best way to reply.

"I don't think so, Paul. The men are very busy. I left so I wouldn't get in their way."

"Aw, please, Terri? I just want to look one time. I won't get in their way. I promise."

"I thought maybe we could finish *Moby Dick* after lunch," she hedged with a persuasive smile.

"But first can we watch? I just want to see for a little bit, is all."

Taryn chewed slowly so she wouldn't have to answer, but Paul wasn't so easily deterred. He skidded his stool back and hopped down. "I want to see!"

"Paul," she cried. "Wait!"

"That lad's one regular ball o' fire, he is," Mary said with a chuckle as Paul sped through the swinging door, letting it bang to and fro behind him.

Taryn pushed away from the counter in hot pursuit. She winced when her hip hit the doorjamb during her flight out the door. The irony of the switched roles didn't escape her. Once she would have been the one to lead her caretaker on a merry chase. Breathless, she rounded the corner of the hallway.

"Easy there!"

Strong hands grasped her upper arms before she could knock down the person coming from the opposite direction. She looked up and barely stifled a groan.

Dan's brows arched in wry amusement. "Out for an afternoon jog, Miss Ross?"

"More like out to catch your son," she retorted. Deciding to forget her former humiliation with this man, she continued, "Paul wants to see them put in the carpet, only Veronica doesn't want him in the way."

"I see." Frowning, Dan turned on his heel and headed toward the room at the end of the hall. Taryn followed, hard-pressed to keep up with his quick stride. Pounding, shushing—the sound of a broom sweeping over wood—and Paul's childish voice grew louder as they neared the open door.

Paul stood just inside, talking animatedly to a burly man unrolling a huge cylinder of olive green carpet with another worker's aid. Across the room, one of the men finished sweeping the floor of debris.

Dan opened his mouth to speak to Paul, then hesitated, his gaze cutting back to the new carpet. "That's not the color we ordered."

The burly man looked up from his task, eyes narrowing. "It's the color on the order."

"I don't think so. My grandmother never would have ordered that. She doesn't like dull greens, and it sure wouldn't look good in here with the rest of the furnishings."

The worker shrugged. "So buy new ones."

A nerve jumped in Dan's cheek. "We didn't order that carpet. We ordered a gold-toned one. A mistake was made—not by us—and it's your job to take care of it."

The man slowly straightened to his feet, eyeing Dan as though he were sizing up a wrestling opponent. He wasn't as tall as Dan, but he made up for it in bulk. Dan had brawn but was leaner in build.

Taryn put a staying hand on Dan's sleeve, certain at any second the two men might come to blows. The other two workers only stood, arms crossed, and watched.

"Call the owner of the shop and discuss it with him," she suggested in an undertone to Dan, her gaze flicking over to

Paul before returning to the rude worker.

The burly man pulled a soiled rectangle out of the back pocket of his tan coveralls and shoved it at Dan. "Here. See for yourself. Number 712. Olive green."

Dan took the paper, unfolded it, and grunted. "You're right. That's what it says. But I still say a mistake's been made."

"Look, bub, I just follow the order form. You got a beef about it, talk to my boss."

"I intend to."

"And while you're at it, take this crazy kid with you. It's impossible to get anything done with him yapping in my face like there was no tomorrow."

Astonished hurt covered Paul's features. Dan's eyes narrowed to slivers of green. He opened his mouth, but before he could speak, Taryn intervened.

"Come on, kiddo." She put her arm around Paul's thin shoulders, steering him toward the door. "You don't want to learn anything from his kind, anyway." She hoped the barb inflicted a sting, but the workman just muttered a reply about ditzy females who didn't know their place, peppering his words with a few expletives that put down her gender.

Teeth clenched to hold her tongue, Taryn moved with the boy into the hall. Paul raced ahead, quickly disappearing around the corner. Dan fell into step beside her, his expression still grim.

"Thanks," he said.

"For what?"

"For preventing a fight. I was about ready to let him have it."

She grinned. "Well, don't paint me into a saint yet. After those last remarks he made, I was ready to give him a bloody nose myself."

A wry smile crept over his face, bringing out his dimple. "Knowing you, I don't doubt it a bit. You're quite a package, Terri Ross."

❧

Now what did he mean by that remark? Taryn positioned the aluminum ladder next to the window in room 201. Dan's parting comment to her after their encounter with the workman days ago niggled at her mind, as it had since he'd delivered it. Had he meant the words as a compliment or an insult? The look in his eyes had been admiring. Almost.

She climbed four of the metal steps and stretched one hand to the top of the heavy drape to unhook it from the curtain rod.

Since their late-night encounter when she thought she'd heard shots, something infinitesimal changed between them. They couldn't be called friends. That was too congenial a term for their relationship. But at least they were no longer at each other's throats like two cats declaring territorial rights. And the past two mornings when Taryn crossed his path, Dan pleasantly nodded her way—no longer looking at her with grim expectancy, as if waiting for her to blow it so he could fire her.

Biting her lip, Taryn tried to lift the third hook from the rod. It remained firmly stuck. Leaning over as far as she dared, she jiggled the metal—and pierced her thumb on the hook's sharp point. Muttering an Irish oath she remembered her mother using on one of her bad days, she stuck her thumb in her mouth, sucking away the drop of blood. Without warning, her eyes lost focus, and the room began to spin.

She grabbed a handful of curtain, but the dizziness robbed her of strength. Teetering, she began to fall and heard the material rip from the hooks. Muffled footfalls hit the carpet, followed by a man's strong expletive as he caught her above the waist—but he was off balance, and they both landed on the carpet.

Taryn rolled away and looked at her rescuer. Dan's green eyes glinted with amusement.

"You know, Miss Ross," he drawled, "we really have to stop meeting like this."

six

Taryn giggled nervously, and Dan winced at his trite remark. He had opted for levity as a defense, hoping to put her on her guard. At the same time he'd hoped to cool the emotions that had begun to brew inside him while he stood at the door earlier and watched her unhook the curtains. Tumbling onto the floor with her in his arms was as fatal to him as boiling oil.

She blinked, and Dan realized she must have knocked her glasses off during the fall. Without thinking he reached out and traced the scar on her temple with feather-light softness. She stared as if transfixed but didn't move away. Tendrils of hair had worked loose from her chignon—and one brushed against his arm, as though to tease him.

Fascinated, he captured the springy red curl, wrapping the end of it around his forefinger, and rubbed its silkiness against his thumb. With a steady but gentle tug of the long spiral, he slowly brought her face closer to his.

The gasp she released was sweet yet sharp—and enough to break through the unseen fibers that had wrapped him with her in some sort of mindless cocoon, where rational thought had no place.

His gaze shot from her softly parted lips, now only several inches from his, to her half-closed eyes. Silently, he reproached himself. What was he doing? Swiftly Dan released the curl and clambered to his feet, almost knocking her over again.

Noticing her equally clumsy attempt to rise, he hesitated then held out his hands.

She stared at him, as if uncertain, but allowed him to help her up. The moment she was on her feet, he let go of her.

After an awkward pause between them, he looked at the ruined curtains and frowned. "Just what were you doing?"

She followed his gaze. "I was taking them down to send to the dry cleaner. Veronica said the budget wouldn't allow new ones."

"Looks like we have no choice now."

"I'm sorry. I got dizzy and fell."

"Dizzy?" Warning bells went off inside his head. "Is this the first time?"

"Well, no. There were a couple of other times since I started working here. But the spells don't last long."

The memory of Gwen's treachery returned to haunt him. "Gram said your appetite has been suffering, too, though I heard that your first morning here you ate like a soldier on leave."

A frown made a V between her brows. "What's that got to do with anything? Some days I eat; some days I don't. Most of the time I'm just not that hungry."

"She also mentioned that you got very sick last week and threw up."

"It was the ammonia we were using. My body reacts that way around harsh chemical smells. Since Mary bought an organic type of cleaner, I haven't had that problem."

Dizziness. Erratic eating habits. Nausea. His jaw tightened as he mentally counted off her symptoms. It was all he could do to get his next words out with a civil tongue. "Miss Ross, are you pregnant?"

"*What?*"

"As your employer I have a right to know."

The look in her eyes suddenly reminded him of winter's ice. "And why should it surprise me that you'd automatically think the worst of me? Tell me, Mr. Carr, do you give everyone such magnanimous benefit of the doubt, or is it only me that you show such kindness to?"

"I'm waiting for your answer."

"No!"

"If you don't tell me, then I'll have cause to dismiss you."

"I mean, no, I'm not pregnant! Satisfied?" Her nostrils flared in indignation. "I've never even—" Her face flamed, and she looked away. "Never mind."

Dan forced himself to calm down. "Okay. Then we need to consider other possibilities." A new thought hit him. "Have you had any nosebleeds since you came to Pinecrest?"

"Nosebleeds?"

He released a weary breath. "Yes, you know. As in sudden and inexplicable bleeding from the nose."

"I do know what nosebleeds are, Mr. Carr. I'm not a total ignoramus."

"I never implied that you were. The only reason I ask is because I think I may know what's troubling you. You're not from these mountains, are you?"

Expression wary, she shook her head.

"Then my guess is that you might be suffering from a case of altitude sickness. I've never known it to last more than a few days, but I guess each individual is different. You'll find if you eat right, get plenty of rest, and don't push yourself too hard, it'll go away. Also, drink lots of water."

He walked to the door and paused, his hand on the doorknob. "Oh, and Miss Ross, one more thing. If I were you I wouldn't climb any more ladders in the near future. I might not be there to catch you next time." With that, he left the room.

⁂

A sharp knock at the door jolted Taryn awake.

Groaning, she rolled over and peered at the clock with one eye open. She caught a glimpse of glowing digital numbers before her eyelid sank again. Thinking she must have dreamed the disturbance, she was almost asleep when the knock came again, more insistent this time.

Muttering under her breath, she grabbed her torn robe from the back of the chair and shrugged into it. Whoever was out there better have an excellent reason for coming to her door at 5:30 a.m. She hadn't slept well. Images of her employer invaded her slumber until she wasn't sure which was worse—the usual nightmares or having Dan visit her dreams. His last parting shot yesterday still infuriated her.

Combing a hand through her messy hair, Taryn trudged to the door and cracked it open. Dan stood on the threshold. She tightened the belt of her robe. "Yes?"

He cleared his throat as though uncomfortable. "Sorry to disturb your sleep, but we have a little emergency. Mary burned her arm and will probably be laid up for the next few days. Her daughter just took her to the emergency room."

"Oh! I'm sorry to hear that."

"Yes, well, we could use your help. Have you ever worked in a restaurant?"

"A restaurant," she repeated. First she was hired to help with renovations, then as a companion for a lonely boy—and now they wanted her to be a *waitress?* "I guess I can pour a cup of coffee and serve a plate of food as well as anybody," she said, still on her guard.

"I take that as a no. Believe me, at this point I'm not picky. As long as you can smile and write an order down, you'll do. Besides Gram, me, and you, there's Mary's granddaughter, Darlene—a sixteen-year-old who might be able to help out after school, if her mom agrees." Dan released a breath of sheer frustration, worry in his eyes. "Gram has taken over the cooking. Too much for a woman her age, but she won't listen to reason and allow me to close the restaurant even for a day. She's not strong—though I'm sure she'd argue the point 'til the sun goes down if I let her."

"Say no more. I'll be glad to help. Just give me ten minutes to get dressed." She hesitated and peered at him from beyond the door's edge. "I won't have to wear a foofy pink shirtdress and a frilly white apron, will I?"

"Foofy?"

"Barbie-doll style."

He grinned. "No. No foofy pink dress for you. Something like what you had on your first day here is fine, though the 'Get a Life' sweatshirt will have to go."

She matched his hesitant grin. "Okay."

Dan shifted his feet in obvious unease. "Miss Ross. . .Terri. We got off to a real lousy start your first day here, and things snowballed straight downhill from that point on. I'd like to try again if you're willing. Truce?"

Taryn eyed his large hand, held out to her in apparent sincerity. It was a nice hand. Strong. Sensitive. With long, artistic fingers and surprisingly clean nails. Maybe if they weren't at odds with one another all the time, she wouldn't think about him so much. She put her cold hand into his warm one. Her heart sped up a beat at the contact, and she pulled away as quickly as she could without being obvious.

"Truce," she agreed.

"I want you to know I really appreciate this—your helping out, I mean. Okay, then, well, I'll let you get dressed, and we'll see you in the restaurant in a few." Before he left, he flashed her a friendly smile—this time robbing her of her next breath.

"In the restaurant," Taryn murmured, watching his lithe form as he strode toward the stairwell. "Right."

She forced herself to move from the door and close it. She must keep focused on the job at hand.

Later, in the restaurant, she actually found herself enjoying her temporary role as waitress. Few customers claimed the tables, but those men who did—mainly residents from town who stopped in for a quick bite before work—were friendly and tipped her well despite her frequent mistakes. Only one man had proved to be irksome. Taryn was beginning to think

Harry Bowers would set up camp in the restaurant, he'd been there so long.

Her glasses had been pinching her nose all morning. Now that the breakfast bunch was gone, leaving only Mr. Bowers, she took them off and looked at them. One of the plastic oval discs that sat against her nose had come off, leaving sharp metal poking into her skin. Great. Now she'd have to locate an eyeglass shop and hope they could fix them cheap, or maybe it would be simplest to find a dime store and buy another pair.

She slipped the glasses into her apron pocket and picked up the ten-dollar bill her last customer had left as a tip, tucking it into the breast pocket of her shirtwaist. To earn extra income, maybe she should suggest that she work in the restaurant during her off time and work only for tips. Both sides would benefit, since the Carrs were obviously having financial difficulties and she needed cash. Her first check should arrive sometime next week.

Ironic that she stood here trying to think up ways of gaining a few extra bucks when she had tens of thousands of dollars buried in a personal bank account in Los Angeles. That account might as well be located on the moon for all the good it did her now.

"Miss—I could use some help over here," the crotchety man at the corner table groused.

Taryn bit her tongue to curb a sarcastic reply, determined not to let him get to her. She'd been forewarned about Mr. Bowers, and forewarned was forearmed as her mother used to say.

Giving him what she hoped was a pleasant smile, she stopped in front of his table. "Yes, sir? How can I be of help this time?"

"The coffee is cold. Can't you people keep coffee hot around here?"

Maybe when you stared into the liquid it turned to ice, Taryn thought waspishly. She was tired of this man and his steady complaints. Ever since he came into the restaurant that morning he'd done nothing but grumble. The service was too slow. The place was too warm. There wasn't enough salt in the shaker. Where were the little slabs of butter he usually was given for his toast? And why were there only strawberry jam packets when he preferred grape?

Taryn knew it wasn't right to make snap judgments, but she didn't like this man, and his features matched his sour disposition. His face was unshaven, his white hair thin and overly long. His craggy features reminded her of Scrooge from Dickens' *A Christmas Carol.* All that was missing was a pair of Benjamin Franklin spectacles perched on the end of his bent nose. His blue eyes under the shaggy white brows pierced her.

"Well?" he complained. She lifted her brow in question, to which he raised his cup off the saucer. "Coffee?" he reminded sarcastically.

"Oh—right." Taryn compressed her lips and went to retrieve the coffeepot. She returned to his table and began to pour, refusing to look at him though his gaze never left her face.

"Say. . .don't I know you?" he asked. "I've seen you somewhere before."

Taryn's gaze lifted to his in shock.

Recognition lit his eyes. "I know! You look like the girl in the paper—"

"Paper?" Taryn's hand jerked. Brown liquid flowed over the gold rim of the cup and onto the table.

"Arrgghh!" Scrooge jumped to his feet, grabbed his napkin, and frantically slapped his lap with it. "What are you trying to do—scald me to death?"

"Sorry!" Her attention went to the folded newspaper by his plate. She could barely see the top half of a woman's face but recognized it as her own. Thinking fast, she set down the coffeepot, grabbed the paper, and sopped up the spill from the table until the print was runny and the pages transparent.

"What do you think you're doing to my paper?" he screeched.

Taryn pushed the soggy mess at him, first ripping the top page away. "Sorry—guess I wasn't thinking." When he made no move to take the paper, she dropped it back on the table. It landed with a moist-sounding *splat*.

"You better believe you'll be sorry. Veronica will definitely hear about this! Mark my words, young lady. You can kiss this new job of yours good-bye."

"Allow me to save you the trouble," Taryn shot back while fumbling with the ties of her apron. She withdrew her glasses, tossed the apron onto the table next to his, and crumpled the damp page of newsprint in one hand.

He blinked. "What are you doing?"

"Serve yourself, Mr. Scrooge. You know how to do things so much better than anyone else in this establishment. At least, that's the impression you give. I quit."

Her short career as a waitress over, Taryn hurried from the restaurant, intent on only one thing.

Escape.

❧

Dan took the stairs to the staff's rooms two at a time. The old man's recriminations concerning Terri sounded in his mind with each step. He didn't blame her for what happened. Harry Bowers was a difficult man to get along with in the best of circumstances. Dan didn't think he'd ever seen him smile, even on his good days. He could imagine the hard time the crusty old man had given Terri, though Dan doubted she deliberately poured coffee in his lap and ruined his newspaper as Mr. Bowers claimed. Dan held back a chuckle. He wished he could have been there when she called the old codger "Mr. Scrooge." He'd thought it often enough.

In the two short weeks since Terri started working at the

inn, Dan saw improvements in his son. Nothing drastic, but enough to make Dan grudgingly admit, if only to himself, that Gram was right and Terri was good for the boy. Her willingness to help at a moment's notice—not only this morning, but other times, as well—spoke volumes on her behalf. The truth was that Dan had never seen an employee as efficient as Terri. Gram was right, as usual. Without just cause, Dan had judged Terri unfairly. And all because of Gwen.

Outside Terri's room, he knocked lightly. Seeing the door ajar, he pushed it open a few inches. "Terri?"

She stopped what she was doing to look up then resumed packing.

Packing? Alarmed, he moved toward her. "If you're worried about your job, let me set your mind at ease. You still have one. I know what happened with Mr. Bowers was an accident."

She quickly folded a pair of jeans in half and tossed them inside the suitcase. Her clothes had been thrown in every which way, and he wondered how she would get the case closed over the heaping, jumbled mess.

"I'm sorry," she said, "but I have to go."

"Terri. . ."

She ignored him, seeming in a big hurry to leave. Dan gripped her arm above the elbow. Her head jerked up in surprise.

"Don't go. I understand that you're upset. We've all had our bad days with Harry Bowers. Gram lets him stay on because she feels sorry for him. He lost his wife and child in an accident years ago and doesn't have anyone else. Like I said, I don't hold you responsible for what happened this morning."

She averted her gaze. "I can't stay."

"Why not? Paul needs you. Gram needs you. I probably shouldn't be telling you this—Gram would have my hide—but she isn't well. She has heart problems and doesn't need this extra stress that's been dumped on her lap. She should take it easy, but try telling her that. She refuses to follow doctor's orders, and I worry about her."

"Heart problems?"

He sensed her softening. "Periods of angina. The doctor warned us that it could get worse if she doesn't take better care of herself and get more rest. We need you at Pinecrest, Terri. Say you'll stay."

"I. . .don't know."

Dan withheld his frustration. He didn't understand why it was suddenly so imperative that she remain, when less than a week ago he was ready to throw her out the door. But it was. And not just because of his grandmother. However, he couldn't hold Terri against her will. "If you want to go, I can't stop you. It'll take time to find another girl as capable as you are, but we'll manage if we have to. I wish you'd reconsider, though. Gram will miss you if you go. And Paul will miss you, too."

He waited a moment.

"I'll miss you."

Her eyes filled with surprise. Dan inwardly winced, wishing he could withdraw the words, but it was too late now. He didn't want her to get the wrong idea and think he was interested in her. Far from it. He just didn't want to lose her as an employee. What's more, Paul regarded her as a friend, and his son didn't have any other friends that Dan knew about.

"All right, I'll stay. But just until you find someone to take my place."

Dan barely withheld a relieved sigh. "Thank you, Terri." Realizing he still held her captive, he released her arm and moved toward the door. "Go ahead and take the rest of the morning off until the lunch crowd hits. You deserve it."

Before she could change her mind, he left.

❧

You've lost it, Taryn. One look into those compelling green eyes of his and you're history. She dropped her head into her hands, digging her nails into her scalp. What had she done? She'd risked everything, and for what? Because a man—who last week she couldn't stay far enough away from—said he needed her help and would miss her if she left.

"Idiot! Idiot! Idiot!" Taryn growled with each item she snatched from her suitcase and slammed into the open drawer. How could she be so stupid? Danger of discovery lurked around the corner—and here she was unpacking her luggage and agreeing to stay?

She glanced into the mirror. Maybe if she did something different to her hair. . . But how different could she go? She'd already endured a pretty thorough makeover at her own hand. She couldn't use color on her hair, couldn't even enter a salon. The chemical smells made her physically ill. Even the acrid odor of nail polish often turned her stomach, but the side effects were minimal since she painted her nails outside. Maybe a black wig? Ebony was all the rage nowadays.

She moved to the window and stared at the blue-shadowed mountains covered with blankets of evergreen. The morning sun dressed the snow with pink and golden highlights in places where the shade didn't fall. This secluded spot was a balm to her troubled soul, and she'd rather not leave Pinecrest if at all possible.

How many newspapers were distributed at the inn? There must be a rack of some sort near the lobby. She didn't remember seeing one, but surely there was one somewhere if Harry Bowers had found a newspaper. She would locate the stand and buy up all the papers left. A mean way to use her tip money, but desperation called for desperate measures.

She withdrew the bills from her pocket and hesitated. Maybe she was overreacting. Not everyone read a newspaper story and remembered the picture accompanying the article. For that matter, not everyone read a newspaper. Sometimes she had a hard time recalling a face after having just seen it minutes before. Unless people were looking for someone or something in particular, they often didn't notice what was right under their noses. Mr. Bowers probably caught on to her because he'd just looked at her picture, right before Taryn came to his table. Maybe if she bought the remaining newspapers and lay low for the next few days it would all blow over.

But what if it didn't? Could she endure the prospect of the media finding her and making her life one of unending misery? Worse yet, other people finding her? People who could destroy her life and force her to tell. . .

Taryn clenched her jaw and moved away from the window, tossing the bills onto the dresser. Her actions were automated as she unpacked her suitcase. The answer to those questions was an unequivocal no. The secrets of that night must remain locked away in the dungeons of her mind. To allow them escape would mean to come forward—and at the same time kill a part of herself, also destroying the most important person in her life.

Taryn looked up at the accusing Bible sampler hanging on the wall. She blinked, feeling hot tears pool in her eyes.

She could never go back. Not until the murder trial was only a distant memory.

seven

Dan stood at the back of the inn and eyed the workers' progress. The light snow that hit yesterday had melted to mush, showing patches of earth in places, and the red mercury in the thermometer hovered several lines above the freezing mark. An unseasonable day, though the chill in the air sharpened with each gust from the north.

While he watched the men work, Dan wondered if this was all for nothing. Mr. Fredericks at the bank had taken a leave of absence and the newcomer filling in for him had denied Dan's application for another loan. Nor had Dan broached the subject to his grandmother about the distinct possibility of having to put a mortgage on the inn.

"Dan! There you are."

He let out an audible groan and turned, forcing what he hoped was a civil smile to his face. "Hello, Laura. What brings you to Pinecrest?"

The slim brunette sashayed her way over to him in high-heeled boots. She was dressed as though she'd just gotten off the slopes, in a bluish green down jacket, black form-fitting ski pants, and a shiny-threaded multicolored sweater that blinded the eye when sunlight hit it. She pouted prettily, cocking her head to the side.

"You're not an easy man to find, Danny. Neither your grandmother nor that new maid you hired knew where to find you."

"I didn't tell anyone where I was going."

"Oh?" Her thick, well-groomed brows sailed upward. "Well, I just wanted to drop over and invite you to the resort

73

for a little ski party I'm throwing Thanksgiving weekend—on Saturday. Just a few close friends, nothing fancy. Afterwards, we'll get together for some food and conversation in the lodge. And Daddy would like to discuss something with you, too. He told me to be sure to tell you to be there."

The news gave Dan anything but pleasure. Bob Grady obviously had discovered that Dan was denied further financial aid. That could mean only one thing. He planned to withdraw his business proposition of the partnership. Unless Dan could convince him otherwise.

With languid grace, Laura moved closer. She put her hand to his shoulder and looked up at him without lifting her head, her brown eyes provocative. "You won't disappoint me or Daddy, will you, Danny? It just wouldn't be any fun without you there."

The concentrated smell of her musk perfume was enough to knock a three-hundred-pound man down for the count. Dan took a step backward, fighting the urge to plug his nose. "I'll have to check my schedule," he hedged.

She broke out into a full-blown smile. "Oh, well, if that's all that's keeping you from committing, then there's no problem. I already talked to Veronica, and she said you had nothing planned for that weekend. So I'll see you then." She kissed his cheek and hurried away, her boots scrunching on the wet snow.

His own Gram had stabbed him in the back. How could she do that to her grandson? Since he was a junior in high school and Laura was in grammar school, she'd had a crush on him. When Dan married Gwen, seventeen-year-old Laura glared at her during the entire reception. Now Dan couldn't help but feel that Laura was sending him obvious signals, letting him know she was hoping to be the next Mrs. Carr.

Dan grimaced. A life with Laura meant fancy parties every month, an annual clothing allowance in five-digit numbers, and constant company with her snobby friends. Besides which, Dan didn't love her. He'd made one mistake with his first marriage, marrying for attraction and not love. He wasn't about to chalk another mark on the loser's side of the matrimonial scoreboard.

Annoyed, he headed for the inn. Before he could walk inside, the door swung open and Terri and Paul almost barreled into him.

"Oh—sorry!" Her words came out in white puffs, fragrant with cinnamon and cloves. She must have just enjoyed a mug of Mary's spiced apple cider.

"My fault this time," Dan replied. "I had something on my mind." When she didn't respond, only stood there and stared, he gave a confused shake of his head. "What?"

"Hmm? Oh, nothing." She turned her attention to Paul and pulled on the boy's mittened hand. "Last one to the creek's a rotten egg!"

"You're going down to the creek?" Dan blurted before they could race away.

"Paul wanted to show me something special he found."

"You can come, too, Daddy," the boy quickly invited.

Dan looked down at his son, then at Terri. Suddenly he didn't want to be left out. "Give me five minutes. I need to discuss something with Gram."

"Okay!" Paul's face glowed with anticipation.

Smiling, Dan tousled his son's dark hair and walked into the inn without another look at Terri. She'd been acting strangely since her coffee encounter with Harry Bowers. Once Mary's daughter and granddaughter came to help, the day after the incident, Terri requested that she be released from any waitressing duties and be allowed to wash dishes instead. She kept to the kitchen when she wasn't with Paul or Gram. On her breaks, she holed up in her room.

For some reason Dan couldn't name, he didn't want her backing out of this excursion now that he'd been invited to go along. Something she might do if given the chance.

He knew he should tell Gram about next weekend now and have her chart it on the calendar before he forgot. He had little choice but to attend Laura's ski party, though he'd almost rather endure a week of jury duty than spend a few hours at one of her extravagant affairs. Still, it wouldn't do for him to alienate Laura's father at this point in time.

On his way to locating his grandmother, Dan glanced into the oval mirror above the brochure table in the lobby. He came to an abrupt stop and looked more closely. A bow-shaped lip print in dark pink branded one cheek.

Muttering to himself, he reached for a tissue from a nearby box and, with harsh strokes, wiped away all evidence of Laura's parting gesture. He wondered what Terri thought when she saw it, then wondered why he should care. He didn't care, he corrected himself. Tired of the mind games his thoughts had played lately, he stuffed the soiled tissue in his pocket and headed to where he'd last seen Gram.

❧

Taryn walked alongside Paul, holding one of his mittened hands while Dan held the other one. They seemed almost like a family enjoying a walk in the woods. Taryn ousted that thought right away. Not a family. Dan was her employer; she was the maid-waitress-baby-sitter, and this intelligent child lumbering between them in knee-high rubber boots was her charge.

She darted a glance at Dan's tall, lithe form. The afternoon sun peeking through the trees gilded his swarthy features while picking silvery blue highlights out of his thick, wavy hair. If he had an eye patch, he would make a dashing pirate. If he could act, Taryn would bet he could have played the role of Captain Kidd far better than the actor her father chose for the part in the film two years ago. Dan had an earthy, male quality—dominant and powerful, yet gentle and seductive—

tempered by that dimple of his. At least the lipstick had disappeared from his cheek. No doubt the woman visitor in the designer clothing had been the bestower of that little gift. Had Dan looked on it as a gift?

Taryn returned her concentration to the path ahead. The last thing she needed was to stumble over one of the mushy clumps of white. Bits of brown peeked from beneath, warning of hidden stumps or logs or rocks, while golden beams of sunlight shimmered to diamonds upon hitting the snow.

At least Taryn was immune to the man's charm. Having rotated in circles of the ultra-handsome and worldly famous taught her that much of the beauty in today's entertainers rested solely on the outside. Taryn wanted someone she could trust. Someone who would help a little old lady across the street without trying to impress. Who would put others before himself and value family more than money. Yet for her to find such a paragon of virtue was laughable. No one of such moral fiber would want anything to do with her dysfunctional family—or what was left of it.

"Why are there frown marks on your face, Terri?" Paul asked. "Don't you like it here?"

Taryn cast a look at the younger male Carr. "Sure I do. I guess I'm just thinking about things I shouldn't."

"Great-Grammy said we should only think happy thoughts," Paul answered wisely. "She said that when we think bad thoughts and don't get rid of them, they can come out in our actions and hurt other people. Is that true, Daddy?"

Dan stopped, as though caught unawares. He glanced at his son and then began walking again. "Gram would know. She's a smart woman."

"She says that Jesus can wipe away all our bad thoughts, if we ask Him to, and give us happy thoughts instead. She called it beauty for ashers, or something like that."

Dan said nothing. Glancing at him, Taryn noticed his

mouth had thinned. Evidently Paul's words found a target. They sure made her feel strange.

"She said when we think bad thoughts about others, we are walking in unforgiveness. And it only makes us bidder. What's bidder?" Paul's eyes sought Taryn's this time.

"Bitter. With a *T*," she corrected. "Like when you bite into a lemon."

Paul burst into a smile. "Oh, I get it! Great-Grammy has a pillow that says 'When life gives you lemons, make lemonade.' She says Daddy bought it for her when he was just a little tyke, 'cause the whole family likes old sayings. What's a tyke?"

Dan's face softened. "A small child."

"Oh. Great-Grammy says that 'the sugar you put in the lemons to make the lemonade is God's love, and that God's love makes even the sourest person smile.'" Paul's brow scrunched in serious thought. "Maybe we should give Mr. Bowers some of that sugar, huh, Daddy?"

For the first time Dan chuckled. "It sure couldn't hurt," he admitted, his gaze briefly going over Paul's head to Taryn. She returned his smile, and for a moment a surge of warmth seemed to pass between them. However, any shared bond was dispelled as a look of tense recognition filled Dan's eyes.

"Paul, how'd you find this place?" Dan's words were coated with disapproval as he came to an abrupt stop and looked ahead.

"I was just playing one day and found it." Paul increased his pace. "It's up here. Come on!"

Taryn wondered about Dan's strange reaction but didn't ask. She trailed the boy down the snaking path, pushing aside snow-covered evergreen branches that blocked their progress and snapped toward her face with a *whoosh* when Paul let go of them. Each time a shower of icy snow sprayed her.

"Paul, watch out—and not so fast," she protested.

The scrunching of boots behind her signaled Taryn that

Dan had joined them. At a clearing, Paul came to a stop and craned his head back. The faint sound of tinkling chimes drifted through the air.

"There!" he shouted, the excitement of discovery making his pitch higher. "Who do you think put those up there, Daddy?"

Taryn looked one-third of the way up a denuded aspen tree. Suspended from a branch, a set of silver wind chimes moved in the chill breeze. She darted a glance at Dan. His face had blanched, and his eyes appeared haunted.

"Are you okay?" Taryn asked.

He swung around in the direction they'd come. "It's time to get back to the inn. Mary's daughter will have the meal ready soon."

"But Daddy—who do you think did it?" The boy ran to catch up with his father. "Isn't this our private properdy, like Gram said? Or does somebody else live here, too?"

Dan didn't break his stride. "No one else lives here." His words were clipped puffs of white clouds.

Taryn looked after them, curious, then hurried to catch up.

Before they reached the inn, with Paul running ahead, Dan stopped and turned her way. "Before you go inside, I'd like to ask something. Would you consider going with me to a small party our neighbor is throwing next Saturday? I need to be there and would prefer to bring someone along rather than go alone."

If he had grabbed her and kissed her on the mouth, she couldn't have been any more surprised. She stood stock-still and blinked, certain she hadn't heard correctly.

"Of course, if you have other plans. . ." Dan frowned when she remained silent. "Maybe you were planning to go out of town to visit family or something—"

"No. No other plans." She resumed her trek through the mushy snow.

Dan was soon beside her. "I'd rather not go, but the girl who's throwing the party is the daughter of the man Gram and I are planning to go into business with. I don't want to risk insulting him, and I might if I decline Laura's invitation. It sure would help me out if you could go with me."

She made the mistake of looking into his eyes. How could they be so soft yet mesmerizing at the same time? "Sure," she said. "I'll go."

"Thanks. You're a real sport to help me out like this, Terri." He nudged her shoulder with his fist as if she were a great guy, gave her a smile, then jogged up the stairs and into the inn.

Taryn stared after him, wondering if she'd just racked up another mistake on her roster of them. Going with him couldn't really be considered a date—more like a friend helping out a friend, though they weren't exactly that, either. And what had there been about those innocuous little wind chimes that made Dan pale at the sight of them? Obviously he harbored secrets, too.

Taryn pulled her hands from her jacket pockets and started up the stairs. She was getting in over her head where her employer was concerned. Trouble was, she couldn't seem to find stable ground, and going with Dan to a party would only drag her in deeper, she was sure. So why had she agreed? Wasn't life complicated enough without adding to the issue?

❧

Thanksgiving swept in with a couple of inches of new snow. The restaurant closed early, and Mary, at the stove again, outdid herself with a huge turkey, basted to golden-brown perfection. The meal passed in quiet camaraderie, though Dan noticed Terri seemed edgy. Gram had asked Harry Bowers to join them for dinner, and the old man sent many a boldly curious look Terri's way. Looks that she avoided.

This afternoon she wore her curly hair so that one side swept over her eye, doing little to reveal her face. He noticed she rarely smiled, though she seemed to be enjoying the meal, and Dan wondered if she were having reservations about tomorrow's party.

"Daniel, do you know what would make this Thanksgiving complete?" Gram's words pricked his thoughts.

"Hmm?" He dished another helping of dressing onto his plate.

"If you and Terri would come to church with me this Sunday."

When he stopped dishing out food and just stared, she quickly continued, "This Sunday is Family Fellowship Day, and the pastor encouraged us to bring our loved ones to the service."

"You know how I feel about long sermons, Gram," Dan said in an even tone, not wanting to hurt her but knowing he had. "I'll take you and drop you off as always, but I can't promise anything more."

"I'll go with you." Terri's voice was both soft and sharp. Dan glanced her way. She looked straight at him, her one eye full of quiet reproach, her lips pulled tight, as though she couldn't believe he would deny his Gram such a thing. But then Terri didn't understand why he resisted.

"Thank you, Terri." Gram's eyes beseeched Dan to give in, as well. But he wouldn't be roped in this time.

"It's a shame about Allison not being able to come," he said, speaking of his cousin who'd planned her Thanksgiving holidays at Pinecrest. "The East Coast sure is getting its share of snow, isn't it?"

"Yes, it is. However, Allison said on the phone that she'd try to switch with another flight attendant and come for Christmas and the grand reopening," Gram said.

"Hey, that's great!" Dan exclaimed a little too brightly. Terri continued to stare at him through the one eye he could see, her mouth pulled down in a frown. He stuffed the rest of a roll in his mouth, grabbed his napkin, and skidded his chair back along the tiles.

"Great meal, Mary," he said, "one of your best yet."

"Where are you going?" Gram asked.

"I should get some work done."

"On Thanksgiving?"

"Holidays—weekdays. They're all the same to me. And the bills wait for no man." He avoided Gram's resigned eyes and Terri's accusing ones.

"We have pumpkin pie and pecan, too," Gram called after him.

"Sounds great. Maybe later."

Without another word, he left the family dining area.

❧

Veronica released a heavy sigh. "Well, then, shall we move to the parlor and dispense with dessert for the moment? I've eaten about as much as I can hold for now."

Paul shot out of his chair and ran around the table to her side. "Can I play now, Great-Grammy—since the room is all ready and the piano doesn't have to be covered up anymore?"

The woman smiled. "Yes, I think that would be the perfect way to end such a splendid meal." Her gaze moved to Taryn. "Spend the evening with us. Listening to Paul play is a real treat. You, too, Harry."

The old man shook his head. "Never weren't much for piano music, Veronny, thanks just the same. I'll head on up to my room and make it an early night. When you get to be my age, sleep is the best entertainment there is."

"Oh, posh," Veronica said, putting her fists to her hips. "You're two years younger than I am, Harry Bowers, so don't give me that excuse. Come now, sit with me a spell."

For a moment Taryn thought she actually saw the old grouch smile. His expression did seem to soften, but he shook his head. "Another time, maybe. Not tonight. Thanks for the dinner."

"All right." Veronica gave an emphatic nod. "I'll hold you to it, Harry Bowers—and you can count on that."

Taryn watched the old man head for the stairs. For someone who claimed to be so tired, he sure had a sudden bounce to his step. Veronica led the way into the lounge, empty now of the guests that would be filling it within weeks. The muted gold carpet the workers had laid blended beautifully with the maroon and gold décor. A wall had been knocked out, making the room larger. In a nook near the fireplace, a small upright piano stood, the plastic protective cover now gone.

Paul headed straight for the small bench and took a seat.

"Why don't you ask Terri what she'd like to hear," Veronica prodded the boy.

Paul looked over his shoulder, his hands on the keys.

Taryn smiled. "Do you know 'Chopsticks'?"

"Sure." He swung back around to the keyboard.

Taryn settled against the comfy sofa cushion, expecting to hear two fingers rapidly strike the keys simultaneously. Instead, smooth, complicated chords emanated from the piano, as the boy began to play like a true virtuoso.

Taryn blinked and leaned forward in shock. Her gaze swung to Veronica's, who eyed Taryn as though she'd been waiting for just such a reaction. The older woman gave a short, unsmiling nod, as though to confirm what Taryn was hearing.

Once the boy finished the piece, Veronica quietly suggested he play something by Schumann. An impassioned melody sprang forth from the keys, at first soothing and gentle, then increasing in volume and intensity as well as speed. Once he finished the piece, Paul began another concerto—this one lilting and bouncy, reminding Taryn of an Irish jig.

"That was lovely, Paul," his great-grandmother said once he finished and the two women clapped their approval. "What was that last piece? I didn't recognize it."

The boy shrugged. "I made it up from things I've heard Mary hum. I'm tired now. My fingers haven't played in a while, and I've got another headache."

Instantly Veronica was on her feet. She moved toward the boy and put her arm around his shoulders, kissing his forehead. "You must rest, Paulie. It's been a big day for you. Ask Mary to give you a children's Tylenol, but only if you think you really need one. The piano will be waiting for you tomorrow if you want to play. Go on to bed now, dear."

Paul looked Taryn's way, his eyes sober behind the glasses. "Great-Grammy told me that when I'm older she'll buy me a grand piano like real musicians use. I can't have one now, 'cause my fingers are too small to spread across the keys. See?" He held out his hands, palms facing Taryn, and wiggled his fingers.

Taryn nodded, feeling awed and somewhat uneasy by the gifted little boy. She'd known from reading with him and joining him in games that he far surpassed the intelligence level of children his age. For that matter, he was smarter in some ways than most adults she knew, herself included.

"Good night, Paul. I enjoyed your music," she said softly.

He smiled. "Maybe when I grow up I'll be a composer like Schumann. Though people said he was mad. . .so maybe I don't want to be like him after all." The smile slipped into a frown, and he left the room.

Long after Paul's sneakers thudded up the staircase Veronica spoke. "Now you know."

Taryn exhaled a long breath, still a bit floored. The boy had played like an accomplished musician who'd been at his career a lifetime.

"His kindergarten teacher suggested I have him tested at a private school for gifted children that she read about. It's in California." Veronica looked at the low, flickering flames in the fireplace. "She said that the curriculum she teaches offers

Paul no challenge, that he's a genius, a prodigy, and that we need to do something about it."

"So why don't you?"

Veronica gave a helpless shake of her head. "Money. Distance. Uncertainty. Maybe a little fear mixed in, as well. Fear that I'll lose my great-grandson to those people who run the school, who are certainly as smart as he is. Daniel isn't in favor of the idea, either. He detests it when Paul's gifts are spotlighted. I have a feeling that's why he chose to work in his office tonight instead of joining us. He knew Paul would play. The boy has been begging to ever since you took the cover off the piano this morning."

Taryn stared into the fire, uncertain of what to think. Was Dan jealous of his son's talent?

"I always knew there was something different about Paul," Veronica mused, "from the moment I saw him lying in his crib. He had intelligence shining from his big eyes, even then. When he was four, he was adding columns of numbers in his head. We'd ask him to put together a large group of numbers—often with more than two digits—and he would give us the equation. The calculator proved his answers correct. I once suggested to Daniel that he have Paul help him add up figures when the office computer crashed several months ago, but Daniel refused."

"I would've never guessed that he's so different," Taryn said. "He seems like such a normal little boy, though I've always known he's ultra smart."

"He *is* a normal little boy," Veronica said in a rush of heated words, so unlike her. She visibly calmed when Taryn lowered her gaze. "I'm sorry, Terri. I get so angry when people—his father included—make him out to be some sort of freak. While he does excel in areas far beyond his age level, in other areas he's as innocent and uncertain as any other child almost six years old."

"And as mischievous." Taryn realized she'd again spoken without thinking and cast a cautious glance Veronica's way. The woman was smiling this time.

"Yes, he is that. Anyway, now you understand. I believe that's why he gets so many headaches and tummy aches and nightmares. Knowing so much, he has more understanding of the way things are in the world, much more so than any child his age should. He even started reading the newspaper this past year."

"He needs more fun in his life," Taryn suggested.

"Which he's getting now with you here. The only reason Daniel sent him to Kinder-Kind in the first place was in the hopes that Paul would mingle with other children his age and make friends. But they consider him an outcast. They won't play with him or have anything to do with him, except to tease him." Veronica reached for a tissue and patted her eyes.

"What about his father? Does he make time for Paul?"

Veronica dabbed under her nose with the tissue then folded it into neat squares. "Daniel loves his son, make no mistake about it. Before Gwen had the accident, he spent a lot of time with Paulie, but after that—" Veronica broke off, sadly shaking her head. "After that he virtually ignored him. Of course, I know what a trial managing Pinecrest has become, but there's more to it than that, I think."

"Oh?"

"Paulie was the last one to see his mother alive," Veronica admitted. "And I believe Daniel blames him for that."

"Blames him? Why? Surely Daniel doesn't think Paul is responsible for his mother's death?" Taryn shook her head, incredulous. "He would only have been around four at the time—right?"

"Yes, that's true. And no, of course Daniel doesn't blame him for Gwen's fall, but, well, you see, Gwen. . .had problems.

Ones that Paulie was a part of, in an odd sort of way, through no fault of his own."

Before Veronica could elaborate, Mary's granddaughter, Darlene, strode into the room. "Sorry to interrupt, but you're needed at the front desk, Mrs. Carr. A man and his wife are having car problems, and they wondered if they could stay for just one night." Darlene grinned, her blue eyes bright. "I think they're honeymooners, with the way she giggles at everything he says."

"Oh my," Veronica said, rising. "At least the plumbing works now. Terri, did you make up the bed and put fresh linens in room 202 this morning as I asked?"

"Yes."

"Good. Since Allison's plane was grounded, they can have the room she would have had."

Taryn watched Veronica bustle away, intent on taking care of her unexpected guests. She couldn't help but feel that the woman was relieved by the interruption. Why? What was there about Gwen Carr that made her—and everyone else—so uneasy? And what could little Paulie possibly have had to do with his mother's death?

eight

Taryn winced, inhaling a hiss of pain.

"Do they pinch?" Dan knelt before her on the spongy carpet of the ski rental shop. "If they do, we'll get you a larger pair. You want boots that fit snug but aren't uncomfortable. You'll never last on the slopes if you settle for less."

"No, they're fine. I bent back a nail when I flipped the buckle." She straightened on the chair and smoothed her index finger over the crease in the quick of her thumbnail. Only one long nail left after this one fell off. She'd lost them while working at the inn, and the polish had chipped away weeks ago. Once she'd been proud of her long nails—real, not false—and changed shades each week, painting them outside near the pool, so the smell wasn't so bad, and often adding little jewels or other decorative embellishments. Such things seemed petty now.

Taryn's eyes lifted to Dan's athletic form. Her gaze met his, and he arched a brow.

"Maybe I should just watch you pros from down here, on level ground. Where it's safe," Taryn muttered. "When you said a party, I didn't know you meant anything like this."

Dan smiled. "Getting cold feet already?"

"I told you. I've never skied."

"And I told you. I used to be an instructor here. We'll start easy and take the beginner's slope. Trust me. You'll be fine."

"Laura might not like it. She's been staring this way ever since I sat down."

Grimacing, Dan grabbed the other boot and slid it over Taryn's thick wool sock. He snapped three buckles into place.

"Laura is the least of my concerns at the moment. Now stand up so I can fasten the buckles at the top." After he finished, he peered up at her. "Can you walk?"

Taryn clomped a short distance in the bulky boots. "If you call this walking."

Dan laughed and stood. "You'll get used to them. They're designed to clamp onto ski bindings, not to parade around in for a fashion show."

"I'm hardly dressed for one, either," Taryn joked, gesturing to her borrowed blue sweater and thick cloth pants that she wore over a pair of thermals. She'd been surprised to learn that Dan's cousin was her size and often left clothes behind from her visits to the inn. Clothes that Veronica insisted Taryn borrow.

Her gaze went to one of the tall windows near the shop's entrance and to Laura, who wore an emerald-colored ski outfit. Even in her ski clothes, Laura looked as if she could fit in with fashion models on a runway. The vibrant woman laughed at something one of her male friends said.

"You look fine to me."

Dan's quiet words startled Taryn, and she turned her head to look at him. But he moved away and began sizing up racks of skis behind an opposite counter. "Just a few more necessities, and you're all set."

Taryn pulled her ski hat farther over her head and watched Dan talk with the employee behind the counter. Her thoughts went to the week-old article she'd read in one of seven identical newspapers she'd bought from the newspaper machine in the front lobby near the restaurant. The news hadn't been good, but that was no surprise. It was that one quote from her uncle, when he was asked by a reporter if he suspected foul play, that bothered her above all else. Uncle Matt had stated, "Taryn will do the right thing. She's always been a good kid and doesn't like to see anyone suffer needlessly."

"Ready?" Dan asked, breaking into her gloomy thoughts.

"If I must."

Dan laughed. "You'll love it. I promise. Here, you'll need these." He handed her a pair of tinted goggles, like his.

Thirty minutes later while Dan took her through warm-up exercises, taught her turns and how to walk uphill a short distance from the lift, Taryn reminded herself of his words to her in the ski rental shop. Her calves ached, as did muscles she didn't even know she possessed in her legs, back, and shoulders. After she got the hang of turning while lifting her skis, he took her to a small hill and showed her how to snowplow, pointing the front tips of her skis inward to slow or stop on a downward slope.

He was patient. Funny. Helpful. The perfect instructor. Taryn surmised that in losing Dan, this lodge had lost a valuable employee. She'd never seen this easygoing side of him, and she liked it. A lot.

"Okay, time to hit the lifts," he said once she'd successfully snowplowed to where he stood at the bottom of the tall mound, three times taller than she.

Taryn's enthusiasm at her success chilled, and she gripped the poles harder. "What? You're kidding, right? I'm nowhere near ready."

He grinned. "You're ready. You catch on quick." With one hand, he brushed the damp hair from her eyes, and Taryn shivered at both the particles of snow clinging to his gloved fingers and the intimacy of the gesture. "Don't worry," he soothed. "The beginner's slope will be as smooth as sliding on glass. The snow is great today. Perfect for skiing."

"Hmph. Easy for you to say. And sliding on glass doesn't sound all that appealing. It sounds painful."

He let out a chuckle that sounded nice to her ears. "Terri Ross, have you always been such a chicken-liver?"

She cracked a smile. "I'm going with you, aren't I? Just lead the way, Dan, and I'll follow."

The words, intended to be flippant, didn't sound that way, and Taryn felt uneasy when she realized that she'd called him by his first name. He stared at her a moment longer, then turned toward the lifts. "The day isn't getting any younger," he said. "Let's go!"

Relieved that he hadn't commented on her hasty words, Taryn awkwardly trailed him to the line for the beginner's lift. When their turn came, she did as Dan instructed and looked over her shoulder to spot the automated chair's approach. The moment she felt it hit the back of her legs, she sat on the frozen metal bench and gripped the side safety bar, keeping the poles across her thighs while Dan did the same and lowered the safety bar over them.

From his place on the double bench chair beside her, he rewarded her with a smile. "You handled that like a real pro. Sure you haven't done this before?"

"Positive," she mumbled, staring down at the white expanse of ground and the people in their colorful winter garb, getting smaller and smaller. The treetops that towered above her minutes ago were almost beneath her feet. She closed her eyes.

"Afraid of heights?"

She sent him a wry glance. "A little late to be asking that, isn't it?" She gripped her poles harder. "It's not the heights I'm afraid of. Just rickety, open-air chair lifts, with only a thin bar between me and a plummet to the earth—which is getting farther away as we speak." She quickly lifted her gaze from the ground and closed her eyes again.

His glove on her arm surprised her, and she looked at him. "Don't worry, Terri. The first time at anything is always a little scary. Just don't rock the chair, and you'll be fine."

"Oh, thanks. That's the first thing I'll probably do now, without even knowing I'm doing it."

He answered with an amused smile and filled in the time by telling her about the variations in snow and how its consistency affected a ski run. Taryn had no idea there were so many types of snow. Wet snow, powdery snow, icy snow. . .

"Okay, now as we approach the platform, raise the tips of your skis," Dan instructed. "When they touch the ground, stand up and push away with your poles—then slide out of the path quickly so you don't get hit in the back of the head with the chair."

Terrific. Something else to worry about. Taryn swallowed hard as the white earth rose up to greet them. When the moment came, she inhaled deeply and did as Dan said, grateful for the supportive hand he put to her elbow. Her legs felt unsteady, but she managed to follow him to the edge of a hill where one of the trails started.

"Good job," he said. "We'll make a skier out of you yet."

She looked down the gradual slope of pristine white. Even the fact that widely spaced pines bordered both sides of the open run and the middle appeared smooth and clear didn't do much to reassure her.

"Come on, you'll love it," Dan urged with a distracting grin.

"Why do those sound like famous last words?" Taryn mumbled.

His laugh warmed her heart. "Just remember everything I showed you, and you'll do fine."

Taryn gripped the ski poles and adopted the starting stance but only stared at the yawning slant of glistening ivory. She wondered what percentage of beginning skiers broke their legs in accidents on their first try.

"Need a push?"

"No!" She took a deep breath, stalling as long as she could. "Uh, any chance we can ride back down in the lift the same way we came up?"

"It doesn't work that way," he said. "Come on, you can brave your Goliath. Just remember what I taught you."

His words arrested her. "Brave my Goliath?"

"A saying of Gram's. She says we all have a Goliath disturbing our lives. We can either face the giant down, like the shepherd David did, or we can stand paralyzed in fear, do nothing, and let him tramp us into the ground."

The word picture brought her own giant to mind, the one she'd been trying to escape for weeks. Taryn forced herself not to think about it.

"All right, fine," she said through stiff, numb lips. With a shaky breath, she anchored her poles to the ground on both sides and pushed off.

The arctic wind whizzed by, stinging her face and robbing her of breath. Icy pellets flew upward as her skis made tracks on the packed snow. She tried to make her legs obey and push her skis into a wedge, but they stubbornly wanted to remain parallel, increasing her speed. Worse, one leg seemed determined to beat the other in a downhill race.

"Balance yourself evenly on both feet!" Dan called from the top of the hill. "Don't lean backward—and push the fronts of your skis together!"

"I'm trying!" Taryn cried before she lost all balance and fell, landing hard on her bottom near the back edge of one ski. She continued sliding. Anxious, she dug her gloved hands and forearms into the snow to halt her progress. Icy granules seeped under her gloves and jacket and stung her bare skin. The poles trailed behind, useless and still attached by the straps around her wrists. She fell back until she lay flat in the snow and came to a dead stop.

Groaning, she pushed her arms and elbows deeper into the snow and forced her upper body upright. One ski lay at a crooked angle, loose from her boot. The other was still clamped firmly to the sole of her boot.

She heard the *shush-shushing* of Dan's skis as he glided downhill behind her. He came into her line of vision with a graceful twist of his body and skidded to an abrupt stop. A shower of snow rained down on her.

"That wasn't so bad," he said with a smile, pulling his goggles away from his eyes. "Ready to try again?"

She glared up at him.

"Come on, Terri. Falling is all part of learning. You just have to learn how to fall. Sitting down was a good maneuver to stop—but next time try to sit on both skis at once."

Pulling her mouth into a tight line, she grabbed a handful of snow, crunched her fingers around it, and tossed the frozen lump toward his face. The pole's strap attached to her wrist impeded her throw and the snowball only hit his pants leg.

"Tsk, tsk. Temper, temper." He had the gall to smile again and jabbed both his poles into the packed snow. "Here, you look like you could use some help up."

She took hold of both of his gloved hands, considered pulling hard on them to make him join her on the frozen ground, then realized if he did fall it would be on top of her. She already felt bruised enough for one day.

Once she was on her feet, he let go. The one ski still attached to her foot felt as if it would take off without her, and she grabbed his shoulders.

"Easy," he murmured, putting his hands to her waist. "I've got you."

A few rapid heartbeats passed before she lifted her gaze from his jacket. His green eyes were tender, mesmerizing. They stood so close that the fog of their breath in the chill air mingled.

"I'll help you get your other ski on," Dan said gruffly after several tense seconds elapsed.

He crouched beside her and clamped the clumsy boot back into the binding. They continued their slow downward trek, but the mood had changed. Gone was the easygoing banter of earlier. Now only Dan's curt instructions filled the awkwardness between them.

Taryn got the hang of snowplowing to break her speed and finally made it to the bottom of the hill, which ended in a natural run-out. To her surprise, she found herself begging to go again. After a moment's hesitation, Dan agreed.

After four more runs on the beginner's slope, Dan said it was getting late. Taryn pleaded for one more run, thrilled that she'd stayed upright on her skis more often than she slid on her bottom—and she was actually having a good time.

"All right," Dan said with a tolerant smile. "But this is the last one."

As the chair lift took them to the drop-off point, Taryn eagerly peered over the mountainside at the majestic groupings of pines, each clothed in soft clumps of puffy sugar-white. The gray-blue of the evening sky painted the background. Over the treetops she caught glimpses of the picturesque town of Pinecrest. From this distance, the brown wooden buildings appeared like a miniature toy Christmas village, with their upright porch beams and slanted roofs garlanded in strings of cheery white lights.

Thwunk!

Above, the motorlike *whir* that accompanied the line of moving chairs ceased, as did the creaks and clicks of running machinery. Dead silence muted the air. Rocking slightly from its sudden stop, the chair lift dangled over what must have been more than fifty feet of space to the frozen earth.

❧

"Great!" Dan muttered. Feeling Terri's anxious stare, he looked her way. "This happens every now and then. It should be fixed soon. Until then, all we can do is wait."

Modifications were still being made to the old ski lift, and Dan wondered if Bob Grady shouldn't have closed it for a season. On occasion, he suspected the man's desire for wealth eclipsed his interest in the tourists' safety. Still, Dan knew that the lift passed a recent inspection, so he assumed everything was in order.

Minutes trudged by, the weight of them seeming like hours. Dan had never been one for small talk, but anything would be better than this heavy, awkward silence that had fallen over them, since the moment on the slopes when he'd almost kissed her.

"How are things going with Paul?" he blurted, uncomfortable by the memory.

The silence broken, Terri jerked in surprise. She seemed hesitant to speak. "I wish I could say everything's fine, but it's not. He seems upset about something." She paused. "I think it has to do with his mother."

The words poured salt into wounds not yet healed. He stared straight ahead.

"Um, I was wondering," she continued. "Do you have any idea why he should feel guilty about her death?"

At this, Dan looked at her sharply. "He told you that?"

"Not straight out, no. But after talking with him, I think he thinks it."

Dan heaved a drawn-out sigh. He'd had no idea Paul felt that way. "To answer your question I'd have to tell you things I haven't told anyone. Gram knows, of course, but few other people do."

She fidgeted with the poles that lay across her thighs. "Oh, well, that's okay. You don't have to. . .I was just wondering how I could help Paul. He's such a sweet boy, and I hate to see him upset."

Dan studied her profile. Today, the spirals of her shining auburn hair were pulled back and fastened with an elastic band at the nape of her neck, and he could see her face clearly. Under the green nylon hat, her smooth brow clouded, as though she were disappointed with his answer.

And he wanted to tell her everything.

Stunned by the thought, he continued to watch her. He'd

never talked about Gwen to anyone since her death, not even Gram. But perhaps here, hanging in a chairlift above a winter-hushed world, with this woman who'd proven to be the opposite of what Dan had first thought—perhaps now was the time to talk about it.

"My wife was mentally unstable," Dan said before he could change his mind. "I didn't realize it until after we married."

Terri stared at him in surprise.

"Gwen and I met in college. Gram sensed something was wrong when I brought her home during spring break. She warned me then not to get involved with her. But Gwen was a knockout—she'd even won a few beauty contests in her area, and I was a fool in love. We married less than a month later. I haven't always made wise decisions, and that was just another stupid one. Even when I hired you, I did so for all the wrong reasons," Dan added as an afterthought.

Terri averted her eyes, evidently uncertain what to make of his confession. Dan quickly continued.

"Gwen met a guest at the inn and spent time talking to her. She began reading books on bizarre religions—cultish-type books. Crystals soon appeared in every room. She even wore one around her neck and never took it off. Fantasy for her became reality. She asked me to put up those wind chimes Paul showed us, and she asked me to put them in the middle of nowhere, because she said then the fairies would hear the tinkling sound and come out to play. She laughed when she said it, so I went along with her crazy idea, thinking it all a joke. At first maybe she was teasing, but later I wasn't sure. It soon became apparent that something wasn't quite right with her. After a while, I began turning down invitations from friends. We never went anywhere because her behavior grew more erratic."

Dan focused on the upright poles of the ski lift ahead, laid out like a row of telephone posts. "After Paul was born, things got worse. Gwen's perception of reality grew completely distorted. She was convinced his genius was a sign that her so-called spirit guides had sent him to her, and she tried to use him as her medium—having him point to things as a toddler, to help her make choices. When he could talk, she asked him questions outright. She often read her bizarre books to him, because she said the spirits told her she must prepare him for the next level he would ascend to."

"Did you try to get help for her?" Terri asked softly.

Dan grimaced at the memory. "Twice. The first counselor was involved in the New Age ideology, too. She scolded me for bringing Gwen and said I was the one who needed to change. Then we took her to a Christian counselor, a friend of Gram's. Five minutes in the room with him, and Gwen became violent, screaming and spitting at him like a wildcat. I couldn't figure out what he'd said that made her so mad—I'd never seen her react that way. I had to physically restrain her. After we left his office, Gwen was hysterical. She cried and held me, begging me not to make her go back. She promised she'd be good and pleaded with me to let her stay at the inn, where she said she was happy. I figured with me keeping an eye on her that home was the best place for her, so I agreed."

Dan hesitated and Terri remained quiet, probably having a hard time believing his fantastic story. It did sound bizarre. But living it had been even more of a nightmare.

"Soon, I began catching her at lies. Small ones at first, then bigger ones. She took things out of my office—important documents, prescription medication, my coin collection—all sorts of things—then lied about doing it, even when Gram caught her in the act. One night she left the inn and found a few local girls in town who shared her beliefs. She spent time with them, sometimes staying out all night. She made travel reservations for exotic locales on our credit card—places she never intended to go. When I discovered the damage, it was often too late to cancel and there would be a charge. I ended up locking away her credit cards and checkbook. Then she started taking money from my wallet, so I had to make sure I always carried it with me.

"She accused me of holding her hostage and started seeing the inn as a prison. At times, she was vindictive, nothing like the gentle girl I married. Other times, her sweet nature would surface. It was like being married to two different women."

He swallowed hard, the next part the most difficult to say. "When Paul was four, Gwen became pregnant again. She wanted an abortion, but I said no. She shouted about her right to choose then days later appeared resigned and told me that she'd changed her mind about having the baby and was going in for a checkup. I offered to drop her off in town, but she told me a friend was picking her up. Later I discovered that Gwen caught a shuttle to the ski slopes and skied the expert run—one of the most difficult trails. They found her twisted body where she'd gone over a drop-off." He swallowed over the tightness in his throat. "She left a note behind, saying that her spirit guide had told her the baby was a mistake, it was time for her to ascend to the next plane, and this was how she'd been instructed to do it."

&

Taryn listened, aghast. She finally understood Dan's mistrust of women—of her. A sickening thought grabbed hold, one she didn't voice. Did she remind Dan of Gwen somehow? Beliefs aside, were they really so different? Gwen had dwelled in a dangerous fantasy world made up of pretense and lies. Taryn also lived a lie, assuming her own sort of pretense—even if it was only to protect those dear to her heart and not for selfish purposes.

The sudden hum of machinery and forward motion of their seat snapped Taryn from her thoughts as the chairlift resumed operation. Before they reached the platform, she had to know one other thing.

"Would Paul have any reason to think he was responsible for his mother's death?"

Dan took a long time before answering but didn't seem surprised by the question. "Paul was the last one to see Gwen alive. From what Gram told me, Gwen spent more than an hour with Paul before leaving the inn that day."

"Do you blame him for what happened to Gwen?"

"No." Dan's reply was swift. "No way. Even if she did seek his advice on the decision she made, he was too young to understand any of what went on. Gwen had a way of talking in circles so that she wasn't easily understood."

"Then why do you resent his intelligence?"

Her question startled him. "I don't resent his intelligence. I fear it. It's a frightening thing to have a small son who's smarter than you. Right now he looks up to me. But one day he'll figure out that his old man's not so smart after all and that he knows a whole lot more than I do."

"Every parent goes through that," Taryn tried to joke. "It's called the teenage years." When he didn't answer, she posed another question. "Dan, do you believe that God is a God of love, like your grandmother says He is?"

He looked away. "I did. Once. Before I knew better."

"What do you mean?"

"I tried to believe for Gram's sake. She talks about a loving 'Abba Daddy God' who remains with His children always. My earthly father ran off before I was born, and then my mother dumped me on my grandparents' doorstep when I was two and took off for parts unknown. So tell me, how can I believe in the God Gram talks about when my own parents didn't even want me?"

Taryn sensed there was still something of the hurt little boy left inside the man, and she empathized with him. She knew how it felt to be abandoned—not physically, but emotionally.

"At least you were raised by grandparents who loved you." Thinking of her own family, she frowned and pushed the memories away. "Maybe your real fear is that Paul will abandon you, too. Is that why you don't spend much time with him? As a sort of unconscious defense mechanism?"

For a moment Taryn thought she'd gone too far. Dan's jaw clenched, and he gripped his ski poles tighter. "I've been swamped with money problems concerning the inn. My distance has nothing to do with Paul."

"Oh?" Taryn's timid question brought no response, and the rest of the ride continued in silence.

nine

Taryn and Dan reached the bottom of the beginner's slope and unclamped the skis from their boots. Laura appeared, with a companionable smile for Dan and a look that shot daggers through Taryn. A tall blond man, with acne-scarred cheeks and a ski outfit that probably cost him a few hundred dollars, stood a little behind Laura.

"My, but you're limiting yourself today, aren't you?" Laura asked Dan as she slipped her arm through his. "You've been on the beginner's slope all afternoon. What a fate for a guy who was once considered an Olympic hopeful! You simply must ski with me on one of the expert runs before we go to the party. I won't take no for an answer."

Dan had the decency to cast a look Taryn's way, showing he remembered her existence. After their silent run down the mountain, Taryn wasn't so sure. Though, to give the guy credit, he had stopped when she'd fallen and waited for her to fumble to her feet.

"Your little maid will be fine. Derrick will take her back to the lodge so she can thaw out. Won't you, Derrick?" She flashed a smile his way then directed her gaze to Taryn. "My, but she does seem to be wearing a lot of snow, doesn't she?" She arched a brow and laughed.

Taryn narrowed her gaze but chose not to say or do anything except to brush what snow she could from her quilted nylon jacket and gloves. Dan gave her a sympathetic glance before Laura whisked him away toward the lift for the expert slope.

The walk back to the lodge was uncomfortable. Were all

the men of Pinecrest so lacking in conversation skills? Obviously the man who clumped alongside her, his thick lips drawn into a pinched frown, wasn't too happy to be stuck with the "little maid." Taryn clenched her teeth. If Laura had known whom she was addressing she wouldn't have been so smug. It almost would have been worth her finding out just to see her face go slack.

Taryn forced thoughts of petty revenge away. How could she so flippantly think of revealing her identity, even for a second, when a loved one's life could be endangered if she did? Death row was nothing to take lightly. She would continue the charade and swallow her pride.

Inside the spacious lodge Derrick led Taryn to the sunken area of the conversational pit where a few skiers, not from Laura's party, gathered. A tall, flocked Christmas tree stood behind a college-aged couple sitting on one of three upholstered sofas. The two were obviously quite in love and unaware of anyone else's existence, staring only at each other. A middle-aged man sat forward on the center couch, facing the huge freestanding fireplace. He stared into the fire's yellow glow but looked anything but happy. His elbows rested on his knees, his hands clutched between them, and a frown puckered his low brow.

"I'll get us some eggnog," Derrick announced to the fire and walked away.

"I'd prefer something hot," Taryn called after him. "Hot chocolate would be nice."

He kept walking, and Taryn wondered if he even heard her. Sighing, she pulled off her knit cap then yanked the rubber band from her hair. With her teeth she pulled off one glove, used her bare hand to pull off the other, then stuck them in her coat pockets and unzipped the jacket. She fluffed her wild auburn spirals over her shoulders. Her actions caught the attention of the lone man, and he looked her way.

Feeling suddenly conspicuous, Taryn offered a vague smile then averted her gaze to the fire, the only place she felt she could safely look. The young man and woman were now engaged in an ardent kiss on the couch. Taryn felt the older man continue to stare at her. Clearing her throat nervously, she considered finding another part of the lodge in which to sit. Would Dan know where to find her if she did?

Derrick returned, two steaming mugs in his hands. Momentary surprise registered across his face when he looked at her. Apparently he realized the little maid wasn't so plain after all, but Taryn had had enough of his kind to last an eternity. Still, she remained seated and sipped her hot chocolate. She listened as he regaled her with pompous stories, making her soon realize that he harbored the wealth to explain away his arrogance.

"Hey, Daddy!" A short young woman with a frizzy haircut trotted across the carpet, catching Taryn's attention.

The worried man shot up from the center couch, his expression angered. "Where were you? I told you I'd meet you here at five."

"Relax. Traffic was bad, and I—" She broke off, catching sight of Taryn. Her eyes widened behind the lenses of her gold wire-framed glasses. "Hey, you look just like the girl on CNN!"

"Gayle, I raised you better than that. Is that what sending you to that fancy college your mother insisted on taught you?"

The woman grinned. "Sorry, ma'am. My father's right. I'm much too outspoken and didn't mean to be rude. But you do look like her."

"That's okay." Taryn pushed the words through a closed throat. "I'm told that often."

"Really?" Gayle gathered her brows in confusion. "I don't see how. The story just aired today."

"What story?" the man asked.

"I guess we all have our doubles," Taryn said with a shrug and stood.

"Where are you going?" Derrick asked with an affronted tone.

"I need to find a restroom. Know where one is?"

Gayle pointed toward the front. "Over there."

"Thanks." Taryn began to walk away.

"I mean it, Daddy. She looks just like that girl they're all looking for in California."

"What girl?"

Shoving her hands into her pockets, Taryn turned the corner. She picked up her pace, walked past the door marked LADIES, and made a beeline for the nearest exit.

❧

Dan left Bob Grady's office, stunned with the job offer Laura's father had proposed once he and Laura returned to the lodge. Being head ski instructor, with a salary to reflect that, would help financial matters at the inn considerably. The one drawback was that he would hardly have any time to spend with his family. When he was home, he'd have to devote almost every waking moment to managerial work. Although, when he thought about it, he was doing that already.

Sighing, he moved toward the conversation pit to join Terri. He hoped she hadn't had too rough a time of it while he'd been gone. Laura wasn't an easy person to get along with, and Dan felt reasonably certain that her friends weren't, either. He'd seen annoyance on the face of Terri's escort when Laura directed him to keep Terri company, and maybe Dan shouldn't have allowed Laura to pull him away. But after the conversation with Terri in the ski lift, he'd been anxious to put distance between them for a while. Terri's words about Paul had hit a chord, making him uneasy.

Entering the sunken area with the fire in the middle, Dan

searched for Terri. She was nowhere. He saw Laura chattering away to a heavyset woman and hesitated. He wasn't anxious to rejoin Laura's company. Matrimonial bells rang too loudly in her head, and he didn't want any part of them.

"Any idea where Terri is?" he asked casually, stopping near her elbow.

Laura spun around, a smile on her face. "Oh, good! I'm so glad Daddy didn't keep you in his office all night. Would you like some spiced cider?" She leaned close, as if to divulge a secret. "It's better than usual. Jim spiked it, and it has a lot more spice now, if you get my drift. Just don't tell Daddy. He still thinks of me as his little girl, though I'm almost twenty-three."

And you act as if you're twelve. Dan looked toward the foyer. "No, thanks. I think I'll go check around for Terri."

The light dimmed from Laura's eyes. "I'm sure she's fine, and you and I have hardly had a chance to talk all day."

"I brought her. I should check on her and see how she's doing."

"Are you looking for your lady friend?" Terri's temporary escort silently moved over the sand-colored carpet toward them.

Dan nodded.

"She left. Said she was going to the restroom but never came back. The desk clerk said he saw her head out the door—walking fast." Frank curiosity was evident on the youth's acne-marked face.

"She left?" A dozen questions clamored in Dan's mind. "Any idea where to?" As soon as the question popped out of his mouth, he remembered what the man said about her asking for the location of the restroom. "How long ago did she leave?"

"Maybe twenty minutes."

"I've got to find her."

Laura nabbed his jacket sleeve. "I'm sure she's fine, Danny. Maybe she wasn't feeling well and decided to return to the inn. It's within walking distance, after all, straight down the road. It's not like she could possibly get lost or anything."

"I still need to check on her and make sure she's all right." As an afterthought, he added, "Thanks for the invite to your party, Laura."

She frowned, but Dan paid little attention to his irritated hostess as he broke away from her hold and hurried toward the exit doors.

&

Taryn trudged near the road through the forest of tall trees. Her mind wavered between the present world and the world from which she desired permanent escape. The past.

Minutes ago, when she'd been walking along the two-lane road, an old sedan full of young men had whizzed past, honking and shouting vile, suggestive things to her out their windows. The incident had rattled her enough that as soon as their red taillights disappeared around the bend she hastened down the small slope, as fast as she could in the rented ski boots. She threaded her way into the trees—but not far enough that she couldn't use the road for a guide. If they came back, she didn't want to be an easy target in their headlights.

Bang!

A gunshot ripped through the silence of night.

Taryn froze, then forced herself to quell her panic. No. . .not a gunshot. Backfire from a car like last time. It had to be. She took slow, deep breaths to steady her choppy breathing and continued at a walk.

Gigantic pines loomed like dark, hulking shadows around her, pointing toward a starless sky. The situation reminded her of that horrible night. With difficulty, Taryn wrestled the specters intent on keeping her trapped in that one segment of time.

A branch snapped, and her breath snagged in her throat. She darted a look over her shoulder.

A dark figure—a man—moved her way from a distance of about twenty feet. Male laughter sounded near the road, and she spun to look in that direction.

"No," Taryn whispered, lost somewhere on a ledge between past and present. Uncertain if one of the young thugs sought her out or if her pursuer was someone she knew—someone who had a lot to lose by what she'd witnessed—she ran deeper into the forest. Her ski boots sloshed through the drifts. The *shushing* of snow sounded extremely loud to her ears.

"Don't run from me!" the man yelled, chasing her.

The words only pushed Taryn harder. But the clunky boots wouldn't obey the speed her brain told her to use. When his strong grip brought her around to a stop, she used what breath she had left to scream.

"Terri!"

In the moonlight visible through the ghostly boughs, Taryn made out Dan's face. Relief almost brought her to her shaky knees, and she reached out to grip his jacket. He caught her and held her close.

"I didn't mean to scare you," he said, his tone remorseful. "Why did you leave?"

Taryn shook her head and pulled slightly away, glancing toward the trees.

"It was something Laura said that made you cry, wasn't it? What did she say to hurt you?"

Taryn was struck by his protective-sounding words. "No. It wasn't anything like that," she said. "I just didn't belong there, and—and I felt I should return to the inn. I'm sorry I left without telling you."

"I didn't belong there, either." His gloved hand cradled her face and her mouth quivered. Warmth pooled inside her, soothing yet vibrant.

"Terri. . ."

Her name on his lips was a whisper, a question. Suddenly

he was kissing her, shocking Taryn. Not with the unexpected-ness of the kiss—for as his lips touched hers, the warmth of their breath uniting, she experienced the sensation of receiving what she'd never known she'd been waiting for. And she returned his kiss as passionately as he gave it.

When Dan's mouth broke away from hers, reality beckoned Taryn to awareness. She placed her hands against his jacket and pushed him away.

They stood, breathing fast, neither saying a word. The one-ness she'd experienced with him blew away as a sudden chill drifted across her heart. He looked as awkward as she felt.

"Terri—I . . ."

"Dan—"

They spoke at the same time, and he dipped his head in a nod. "You first."

Taryn wished he had taken the initiative. What could she say to explain her erratic actions—blowing hot, then cold? "I think we should be getting back to the inn. It's late, and I'm freezing." She shouldn't have added the last. Would he try to put his arm around her on the walk back and hold her close to his side? Could she stand it if he did? Or would she melt and wind up telling him things she shouldn't?

He stared at her a few seconds longer before replying. "You're right. It is late. Later than I thought." The words seemed to hold double meaning, but the smile he gave her was polite enough. "Is there a reason that you were walking in these woods and not near the road?"

Taryn grabbed the change of topic like a rope to tow her out of deep water. "There were some boys in a beat-up sedan—out joyriding, I guess. They called out to me when they drove by, and I just got a little spooked."

"Jim Perrow's kid with his delinquent friends." Dan's voice was grim. "They're harmless enough. All talk, no action."

Taryn wasn't so sure. She was suddenly glad for Dan's

presence beside her. Yet as they walked back to the road, his words of censure clamored in her head. "Delinquent friends," he called the tough youths. And so they appeared. Yet if he thought those boys were bad apples, what would he think of her dysfunctional family? Of her? As much as she might wish it, she could never tell him the truth: that compared to her relations, those "delinquents" were Boy Scouts. And she wasn't exactly Girl Scout material, either. Not now, since she was running from everybody and everything she knew; since her life these past six weeks was based on a lie; since she was wanted by the police. . .

"We're more than halfway to the inn," Dan said, interrupting her train of thought. "To go back for the truck seems pointless. I'll pick it up tomorrow."

The walk back was mostly silent, punctuated by forced polite words every hundred yards or so. The tension between them blew as stiff and cold as the frosty air chilling Taryn's face. When the welcome glow from the inn's windows came into view, she was hard pressed not to break into a run, away from Dan, and find solace within her room. Yet once they walked through the door she sensed something was wrong. Harry Bowers ambled forward, as quickly as his arthritic limbs would allow. Remorse etched deep wrinkles into his craggy face.

"Dan, If I'da known he woulda taken on so, I never woulda said what I did."

"What are you talking about?" Dan asked. "Where's my grandmother?"

"Veronny's up there with Paul, trying to get him to come out." Taryn had never seen Mr. Bowers look so ashamed. "The boy got in my room somehow and tied all my socks together in a rope. My joints were flarin' up—it's so hard to use these old hands anymore—and when I saw what he done, I let him have it. I yelled some things I shouldn'ta said. . . ."

Dan didn't wait to hear more. He headed for the stairs and took the steps by twos. Before taking off after him, Taryn glanced at the man, who seemed to withdraw into himself, making him look older and smaller. She pitied him, but her first responsibility was to Paul. Even before she rounded the corner of the stair landing behind Dan, she heard crying coming from within one of the rooms.

Relief softened Veronica's haggard features, and she moved away from the closed door of an unoccupied guest room. "Daniel, I'm so glad you're back. He ran in there about twenty minutes ago. I've tried talking to him, but he won't come out."

"Let me try." Dan moved toward the door and lightly rapped on it. "Hey, bud, how about letting me in and telling me what this is all about?"

"I—I can't. . . ." Sniffling and hiccupped breathing accompanied the reply.

"Sure you can. Let's talk about what happened. We can work this out, but you have to open the door so we can talk about it man-to-man."

"No. . . ," the trembling answer came back.

Taryn moved forward, hoping she wasn't interfering. "May I try?"

Dan seemed surprised to see her, as if he'd forgotten her presence. He gave a curt nod and stepped away from the door. Taryn claimed the spot where he'd stood. Dealing with children wasn't her specialty; she had so little practice at it, but she'd learned enough about Paul these past weeks to hope she could get him to respond favorably and open the door.

"Hey, Paul, I missed you today. Actually, I'm not all that sleepy, so if your Daddy and Great-Grammy approve, I'd like to read with you before you go to bed. We were starting *Oliver Twist*, if I remember right. Did you know they made a musical of that story? Maybe sometime we could rent it and see it together."

Sporadic sniffles met her suggestion.

"I really hate having a door between us, Paul," Taryn tried again. "But I understand how you're feeling, because I had a bad thing happen to me today, too, and it upset me. Friends tell each other when things are bothering them. It helps. If you'll let me in, maybe we can do that—tell each other what's bugging us—and then we can ask Mary to make us some hot cocoa, and read a few chapters in that library book."

"Just you," his tiny voice came back after tense seconds passed. "Nobody else."

Taryn looked up, and Dan nodded again, though she detected the hurt in his eyes.

"Okay." She leaned closer to the painted white door. "Just me."

A lengthy pause ensued before the lock gave a faint *click*, the knob turned, and the door swung inward a fraction. Paul stared out the crack, a much too somber look on his features for a boy of almost six. His glasses were missing, and his face bore red, blotchy patches. The sight of his woebegone expression almost brought Taryn to her knees in an instinctive motherly action—to hold out her arms to Paul and comfort him. Yet she held back, sensing that such a display wouldn't be received well.

"May I come in?" she asked.

He disappeared farther into the room. Taryn took that as an invitation to follow, and did so, leaving the door cracked open.

The room he'd sought refuge in was still being remodeled, and Paul sat on the edge of the bare mattress. Taryn wondered how he'd gotten the key since all the guest rooms were kept locked, but with his cleverness and resources, it probably hadn't been too difficult.

Taryn took a seat beside him, placing her hands between her knees so as not to give in to the impulse to wrap the little fellow in her arms.

"Why don't you go first," she said. "Tell me what's bugging you."

He gave a world-weary sigh, his gaze fixed on the carpet. "Mr. Bowers doesn't like me. I tied his socks together in knots for fun, and he yelled at me and said I was crazy like my mother." Paul looked down at his brown corduroys. "He said she never cared about people's feelings neither, and that nobody liked her."

Her heart twisting, Taryn searched for appropriate words. She was thankful she knew about Dan's wife, so she could better understand how to deal with the situation. But how much did Paul know? Was he aware of his mother's suicide?

"Paul," she started slowly, "sometimes people say things they don't mean when they're mad, and Mr. Bowers was very mad. I don't think you're one bit crazy, and I like you a lot."

His mournful expression remained. "I wish I could be Ceddie in *Little Lord Fauntleroy*. Everybody liked him. . .and in that movie, at Christmas, he even got his mama back." The last words were spoken in a whisper, but they tore at Taryn's heart, and she gave in to the urge to put one arm around his drooping shoulders and squeeze tight.

"If you'll remember, his grandfather didn't like him all that much at first," Taryn replied quietly. "In fact, the earl was a lot like Mr. Bowers. But the thing that made Ceddie so likeable was that he earned his grandfather's love—and everyone else's—by being kind toward him and others. By putting others first. That's why he was so popular."

"It wouldn't matter anyway. Even if I was like Ceddie and was good all the time and didn't play pranks and people liked me. 'Cause Daddy would still hate me. I should've died with Mama."

Shocked, Taryn swung her gaze from the carpet to his bowed head. "Paul, of course your daddy doesn't hate you! Why would you think that?"

"He thinks I'm crazy like Mama. She was going to take m
with her that day she had the accident—I remember. She pu
on my overcoat and boots, but my head hurt so much and
was crying, and she got mad and left without me."

The revelation that Paul could have been a victim o
Gwen's deranged reality was startling. Knowing that tw
could have died that day instead of one, Taryn hugged Pau
more closely to her side.

"I think Daddy wishes I'd gone with her. He thinks I'n
crazy, too. That's why he doesn't ever want me around or wan
to play games with me or anything. I guess geniuses are al
crazy."

Suddenly the door swung open all the way, and Dan cam
into the room. The look of remorse on his face and the shin
of tears in his eyes halted whatever Taryn was going to say
and she dropped her arm from around Paul. In a few quic
strides Dan was beside the bed and kneeling in front of hi
son, who looked at him with a mixture of wariness and frigh
as though certain he was about to be punished for what he
had said.

"Paulie, can you ever forgive me for making you feel tha
way? I don't think you're crazy, and I certainly don't hate you
I may not say it enough, but I love you, buddy." He put hi
arms around the boy and brought him close, the tears now
trickling down his cheeks. Paul wrapped his arms around
Dan's neck as if he'd never let go.

Taryn felt a catch in her throat as she watched. A strong
need to belong to this family, to have the right to put her
arms around both of them, mushroomed within her, putting a
pain in her chest. But she didn't belong. Would never belong
Not to them. Not to anyone. And the reminder wedged
another thought into place: She should leave Pinecrest before
it was too late.

Now feeling like an interloper, she quietly left the room.

ten

Fidgeting, Dan tried to relax on the cushioned bench beside his son, with Terri on the other side of him. To everyone's surprise, Mr. Bowers also had made an appearance at the little stone community church and sat beside Gram on the other side of Paul. Dan enjoyed having his son nestle close to his shoulder, but unease ate away at his gut.

Last night after Paul hugged him tightly, he had asked, with wide innocent eyes, "Will you come to church with me and Great-Grammy tomorrow, Daddy?"

Dan had felt cornered. He couldn't refuse. Work had become top priority in his life ever since his grandfather's death, but even more so after Gwen's suicide. Though Terri spoke of her concern regarding Paul, Dan hadn't realized how much his distance was harming his son. Not until he heard Paul's shaky words on the other side of the door, words that shocked him into awareness. So how could Dan refuse the boy's simple invitation to attend church with him this morning?

"What you have to get hold of is the fact that you're not responsible for the actions of your loved ones," the pastor said from the pulpit.

His attention roused, Dan shifted his gaze to the front of the church and the flush-faced preacher. Now the short man paced back and forth as he eyed his congregation. Sweat glistened on his high brow.

"Everyone has his or her own choice to make," the pastor went on. "If you tried to help someone and they wouldn't listen—or, parents, if you trained your children in a Christian manner and set a good example, but they wouldn't have anything to do with it, and they wound up choosing a different road that led to sin—then you can't go on beating yourself up over their decisions. That only puts a person in chains of guilt. 'What could I have done better?' 'If only I'd done this or that or the other. . . .' People, the truth is, God doesn't hold you responsible when others fail, especially if you tried to prevent their downfall."

Earlier, Pastor Trent announced that the original teaching he'd planned had been preempted by a message he thought the Holy Spirit wanted to impart. And now Dan felt as if the rapid words were being directed with arrowlike precision to his heart. Sensing Terri go rigid, he turned his head to look. Her brow was furrowed in a deep frown.

"Rather, it's your own attitude and decisions that God holds you accountable for," the preacher continued. "Despite what others might do or how they might hurt you, God looks at your attitude and how you respond. But the best news is that He's there to show you how. He knows it's difficult to keep a good attitude and make wise decisions in this world, to be righteous as He is righteous. He once walked this earth, too, and faced just as many thorny people and situations. Since He's traveled the road before us, He's promised to be a guide for us—when we ask Him. But only if we ask Him." The preacher quieted, and his eagle gaze targeted Dan's row. "God doesn't want His people to live a life of bondage, hampered down by guilt or an unforgiving attitude. He wants them to live a life of peace."

"I'll be back," Terri mumbled. She silently rose, edged past an older couple, and quickly walked toward the back of the A-framed church.

Dan wondered if the message affected her as deeply as it did him. If Paul wasn't asleep against his shoulder, he might also rush out of the sanctuary, away from the convicting words.

While the preacher continued his message, Dan did self-inventory. Yes, he'd blamed himself for his mom dumping him on Gram's doorstep, sure there must be something wrong with him that she wouldn't want her own son. And he'd felt guilty for Gwen's death, deciding he must be the worst kind of husband for her to do what she'd done. He'd also felt in some way responsible for her mental illness. In self-defense he exhibited a sour attitude toward every young woman he encountered, unfairly judging them. Including Terri, who'd proven her worth and reliance a million times over. He had hurt her more than once with his sharp words and mistrust.

Well, no more. From now on he would do what he could to make it up to her. Not all women were like his mother or Gwen. In fact, maybe, just maybe, he could trust his heart to take the lead, and tell Terri how he felt about her. He would like to try to trust a woman again, if that woman was Terri. He enjoyed their day on the slopes, even if he'd become annoyed at what he considered her intrusion into his affairs concerning Paul. But she was right. The pretty redhead, who tried so hard to downplay her looks, had been right on target. She was smart. Attractive. Compassionate. And he was lonely for a companion.

Dan relaxed against the bench, deciding to put his plan into effect that night.

સ

At Dan's summons from Paul, who stood in the hallway and giggled as if he had a secret, Taryn set down her book and followed the boy downstairs to the parlor.

"Get your hat and coat," Dan said when he saw her, not a flicker of emotion on his bronzed face.

Taryn stopped mid-step, dread hitting her. Was this a dismissal? But what had she done wrong?

Last night, she had tossed around the idea of leaving, especially after what happened at the ski lodge when her cover

was almost blown. However, she came to the conclusion tha
if she remained at the inn and never visited the resort agair
she'd be safe. Veronica's weak condition convinced Taryn t
stay, and the elderly woman hadn't looked at all well thi
morning. Although she smiled widely to see both Dan an
Taryn accompany her to church, not to mention the gruffl
silent Harry Bowers, Taryn sensed the woman felt ill. Sh
couldn't leave her employers in the lurch, as the maid befor
her had done. Not when she'd promised to help them reacl
their goal of reopening the inn at Christmastime, four week
away. But had the decision to stay been wrested from her?

Dan chuckled. "No need to look like that. I'm not throwin;
you out on your ear." His eyes gleamed. "Go get your thing
before the horse takes off without us."

Horse? Taryn threw him a confused look then swung he
gaze to the others. Veronica was beaming. Even Mr. Bower
looked as if he might actually crack a smile.

"Hurry, Terri," Paul urged from behind her on the stairs
"Daddy said when you get back, he might take me."

Get back? What was going on here? Yet instead of voicin;
her curiosity, she did as everyone expected and went upstair
to bundle up in her long wool coat, stretchy hat, and cloth
mittens. Dan smiled his approval when she returned to the
foyer. As he opened the door, she heard what sounded lik
sleigh bells. *What on earth. . . ?*

She stepped off the snow-dusted stoop, halted, and then
clapped her gloved hands together in childish delight. A
mocha brown horse was hitched to an open sleigh furnished
with a thick fur blanket. The horse tossed its black mane
causing the silver bells on the harness to jingle in the frosty
air. A ruddy-cheeked driver in a checkered coat sat on a
bench seat and nodded her way.

For a moment Taryn almost forgot herself. She whirled
toward Dan, her mouth opening to offer thanks for the

unexpected treat. Noticing how his eyes gleamed—with what? hope? anticipation?—Taryn paused.

Taking this ride with Dan might not be wise. Her heart was already drawn to the man. Once she stepped into that sleigh and snuggled under the blanket beside him, she sensed they would approach an inevitable crossroads in their relationship, one in which she must make a choice. Nothing could be the same again. Or she could play it safe and refuse, by offering some sort of excuse, and return to the house and safety.

The magnificent horse snorted. Puffs of frosty white billowed from its nostrils and into the air. Dan held out his hand to her. Taryn took it.

One night, she argued against the sound reasoning that struggled to be heard in her mind. *One night I'm going to live in this idyllic dream with the man I love beside me.*

There. She admitted it. She loved Dan. And his family. It didn't matter, though. Her love wouldn't matter one whit when reality's stark truth shattered the dream and he discovered who she really was. Such an event was inevitable; she knew that now. She couldn't hide forever. Though, hopefully, when he did learn the truth she would be long gone from here. But for this one night, just this night, she dared to live the dream.

Taryn relaxed against the red leather seat. The runners swished over the crisp snow, and the bells jingled, heralding their arrival to the skittish rabbits and squirrels that Taryn glimpsed darting into the thick forest. A fading sunset tinged the snowy world around them rose pink.

She sighed contentedly. "Oh, Dan. Thank you for treating me to such a wonderful surprise. I've never been on a sleigh before."

He grinned. Under the blanket pulled over their laps, he covered her hand with his and gave it a squeeze. "Another first for you?"

"Yes. It's all so beautiful and Christmassy feeling."

The conversation between them was light, the topics care-free. Mostly about Christmas and the pre-opening party that Gram was planning. After a brief interlude of quiet, Dan grew serious.

"Terri, I never thanked you for what you've done for Paul and for being such a good friend to him. I should thank you for what you've done for me, too. Your wise words helped me see what I was doing to my son, and I'm grateful."

Taryn nodded, basking in the warm glow of his approval.

"But it's more than gratitude I feel toward you," he added quietly. "Since the day you first walked into my office, you've exasperated me, amazed me, and puzzled me. But you've also made me feel emotions I never thought I could feel for a woman again. I think I'm falling in love with you, Terri Ross."

He lowered his head the few inches needed for their lips to touch. She pressed against him, closing the last bit of dis-tance. His kisses were warm, sweet, going to her head like a fine wine.

Could she make the dream last a little longer than one night?

≈

Dan entered the front room, a mug of steaming black coffee in his hand, and grinned when he saw Terri. She stood to one side of the Christmas tree, humming along with the Perry Como tune crooning from the speakers. Festooned with necklaces of colored-tinsel garland and sporting a few mis-placed silver icicles in her hair, Terri matched the song.

Dan set his mug on the piano, moved with catlike silence, and came up beside her. She paused from tucking a long rope of blue tinsel between the pine boughs and turned in surprise. He captured the dangling end of the green tinsel that lay wrapped in slack loops around her neck. Giving the crackly strand a gentle tug, he brought her closer.

"You're the one who's beginning to look like Christmas,"

he murmured before depositing a kiss on her lips. They tasted
of hot chocolate and sugar cookies. "Mmm. . .and you taste
like Nestlé's bakery." He would have deepened the kiss, but
she put her hand to his chest and moved back slightly, shaking her head and smiling.

"Paul's on the other side, by the window," she whispered.

Dan released a poor-me sigh, matched her grin, and con-
tented himself with one more brush of his lips over hers
before dropping the tinsel.

"Hey, buddy," he said, moving to the opposite side of the
tree. "How's it coming?"

Paul pushed his glasses higher on his nose and screwed up
his face in a scowl. "Why'd we have to get such a tall tree,
Daddy? I can't get all the tinsel up there."

Dan looked toward the top. In a few spots the tinsel lay
clumped on the branches, as if Paul had thrown it up there in
desperation. Seeing a number of narrow silver strands litter-
ing the carpet, Dan assumed that had been his son's method
of choice.

"Well, now. I knew I was six-foot-four for some reason."
Dan slid his hands beneath Paul's arms and lifted him high.
The boy squealed in delight, then quickly sprinkled tinsel bits
over each branch.

"Where's Great-Grammy?" Dan asked after he set the boy
down.

"She said she was tired and went upstairs to lie down," Paul
said matter-of-factly.

Alarm pierced Dan. If his grandmother had gone to rest of
her own accord, then something was definitely wrong. He
thought back to the many times he'd urged her to take it easy
and she had brushed his comments away.

"She and Mr. Bowers took a walk earlier," Terri said, coming from around the other side, her concentration again on
her task. The green tinsel was missing from her neck and

now bunched in her hands as she threaded and looped i'
through the boughs. A delicate colored bulb shook then fell
Before it could shatter to the flat carpet, the hook caught on
a row of gardland. Terri breathed a relieved gasp, plucked i'
up, and set it back on its high branch. "I wouldn't worry. She
was absolutely glowing when she came in. Their walk was a
long one, and she decided to take a nap before supper."

"Speaking of glowing, you're doing some of that yourself,"
Dan said as he pulled a silver strand of tinsel from her hair
"You really enjoy all this decorating hullabaloo, don't you?"

She nodded. "Christmas is my favorite holiday."

"I like it, too. Though I'm not much into the decorating
part of it. I like the company it brings though." These past
two weeks with Terri had been fun and satisfying, though he
wanted more. He sensed she did, too, but felt her resistance.
He wondered what she would do if he proposed on the spot
instead of waiting until Christmas as he planned.

Her silvery gray eyes shimmered as brilliantly as the tree's
icicles, while electric seconds passed between them.

"Aw, you're not going to kiss her again, are you?" Paul suddenly blurted, making them both jump in surprise.

Terri blushed, and they both laughed self-consciously. "Can't
put anything past him, can we?" Dan asked in a low voice.

"Will you put the electric twinkle-star on top now, Daddy?
You're the only one who can reach."

"I will, but not tonight. Great-Grammy wouldn't want to
miss that. Besides, she prefers to do the star on Christmas
Eve. I don't want to break tradition."

"So I have to wait five more days?" Paul asked with a groan.

Dan smiled. "They'll fly by. You'll see."

"Then can we go for a walk?" Paul's little fingers circled
Dan's wrist. "All three of us?"

Terri's hopeful expression showed how much the prospect
appealed. "I should finish decorating this room," she said. "I

told your grandmother I would."

"Walk with us," Dan coaxed. "I'll help you when we get back."

"I thought you weren't into decorating."

"I'll make the sacrifice."

She grinned, her manner almost shy. "Okay."

While Paul scrambled to his room to get his overcoat and boots, Dan walked with Taryn to where her coat hung over a chair near the fire. The navy wool was still damp from their snowball fight earlier that day. As he held the coat open for her, he noticed one of the triangular buttons missing from the cuff and casually pointed it out.

Frowning, she brushed a finger over the loose black threads and shrugged. "I must've lost it in the snow. It's only there for decoration, so it's no big deal."

Still the lines remained between her eyebrows. Dan kissed them away then sneaked another kiss to her lips before his eagle-eyed son could catch them in the act.

≈

Snow fell with dusting-powder softness to add another layer of cottony white to the trees. It covered the hollow footprints Taryn, Dan, and Paul made earlier as they'd strung lights around windows and over the bushes of the inn. Taryn leaned her forehead against the chilled pane and watched the blue, pink, and green lights twinkle in cheery welcome.

Somehow, she'd made the idyllic dream stretch out for three wonderful, indescribable weeks. Dan had joined her in work, and together they painted, hammered, and shifted furniture around the inn. In between they decorated, teased, and romped over the snowy grounds like two big clumsy kids. Taryn knew it was only fair to Dan to tell him the truth. Yet every time she opened her mouth, intending to do so, she caught the gentle look in his eyes, the way his sensitive lips pulled into a boyish grin, and just couldn't do it. She couldn't kill his newfound joy. Horror was sure to cross his face when he discovered the truth. Then hate. And revulsion.

Now that the inn was refurbished and ready to receive guests, maybe it was time for her to disappear. Like the fragile snowflake drifting to earth to lose itself and blend into a sheet of white. Maybe it was time for Taryn to leave this remote area and find another town in which to hide.

"There you are," Dan's puzzled voice said from behind. "What are you doing in here? The guests will be arriving any minute."

Taryn looked over her shoulder. "Just grabbing a few quiet moments before the party starts."

"If you're worried about Laura, don't. She won't act up with her father around."

Taryn lifted a brow. "You sure about that?"

The hum of voices in the front lobby announced the arrival of Gram's guests. Hearing Laura's high-pitched welcome, Dan grimaced. "Guess we'll find out." With one arm he drew her close and kissed her temple. "Just keep reminding yourself that this'll all be over in a few hours and she'll be gone."

"This too shall pass?" she asked, quoting one of Veronica's wall samplers.

"I sure hope so."

Taryn giggled. At the sound of heels tapping along the hallway, she tried to push away from Dan, but he tightened his hold. They both looked toward the entryway.

Laura swept into the dim room, her calf-length black leather coat flapping about her. Only the Christmas tree lights twinkled and one table lamp glowed in the corner. Her brows lifted in curiosity, but her dark eyes glittered. "Well, isn't this cozy?"

"Laura," Dan acknowledged with a nod. "Glad you could make it."

"Are you?" Her gaze shifted to Taryn, narrowed, then swung back to Dan. "Well, maybe you won't be when you see what I've brought. Please understand, though, that it's for your own good I did this. It's only because I care. I don't want to see you manipulated again, Danny."

A trickle of apprehension ran through Taryn. "Maybe you should save this for later, and we should join Gram and the others now. Mary's worked so hard to prepare the food, and Gram's been looking forward to this night for weeks."

"Oh yes, you'd like that, wouldn't you?" Laura's voice dripped venom. "If I weren't a guest here tonight, I'd scratch your eyes out for what you've done!"

"Laura!" Dan exclaimed in outrage. "That's enough."

Taryn tugged on his arm. "Dan, please, let's just go—"

"She lied to you, Dan. To all of you."

Taryn felt his arm tense and go rock-hard. He made no move to leave, and when she tried to step away, his fingers dug into her waist. "I think you'd better apologize, Laura. Otherwise, I'll have to ask you to leave my home."

Laura flinched as if wounded. Desperation pooled in her eyes. "She's really got you fooled, hasn't she? But facts don't lie." As she spoke, she extracted a piece of paper from her shoulder bag, unfolded it, and thrust it toward Dan's face.

Underneath Laura's shiny red fingernails, Taryn eyed the computer news printout of her smiling face next to a photo of Pat's, and then one of her father's—with the bold headline beneath:

MURDER TRIAL PENDING FOR BAD-BOY
SON OF SLAIN HOLLYWOOD DIRECTOR;
TWIN SISTER AT LARGE.

The idyllic dream shattered into thousands of sharp, unforgiving pieces. Dan dropped his hold from around her waist and turned horrified eyes her way. Taryn could only shake her head, her own eyes misting, then run, stumbling, from the room.

eleven

Taryn threw her clothing into an open suitcase. This time she was leaving. Dan wouldn't want her to stay. Gram probably hated her, too. Worse yet, Laura might have already called the police. The police!

The sudden thought doubled her speed. In her haste, she bent back a half-grown nail and muffled a cry. She popped the injured finger into her mouth. A knock sounded at the door, which she'd left ajar. Mary pushed it the rest of the way open.

"Might I talk with you for a moment?" she asked.

"I haven't got time. I'm leaving."

"Please." The cook's blue eyes were beseeching, even hopeful, as she stepped into the room. "You're Taryn Rutherford? Megan Rutherford's daughter?"

Taryn tossed her nail care kit into the suitcase and looked up in shock. "You knew my mother?"

"Aye." Mary gave a hesitant smile. "We went to school together in Ireland. It was your mother I came to visit so many years ago. But I'd heard she died."

Taryn nodded.

"Ach, I am sorry. Your mother was a gentle spirit, but a wee bit wild. She married Charles to get away from Ireland. . . ." She paused, as though concerned she might have said too much, and withdrew a packet of tied-together envelopes from the pocket of her Christmas apron. "She wrote me every holiday. Long, newsy letters. Ones that bared her soul. She had no one else to talk to."

Taryn again nodded. Her father never had been great on communication, except toward Hollywood's starlets.

Mary handed over the thick packet of letters. "I want you to have them. She would want them to go to her daughter." She smiled in wistful remembrance. "You have her beautiful hair."

Taryn eyed the packet of letters, and tears sprang to her eyes. How many times had she wished to know her mother better? To know her at all? She remembered so little about her. Heavy footsteps in the hall alerted her to the present danger, and she snatched the letters from Mary's hand and stuffed them inside her suitcase. "Thank you," she blurted. "But I have to get out of here now." She snatched up her books from the nightstand and threw them atop the clothes in her suitcase.

"I owe your mother everything," Mary said quietly.

Dan's presence suddenly blocked the door. Mary looked between her employer and Taryn and hastened to the exit. Arms folded across his broad chest, Dan stepped aside to let the heavy woman pass, then resumed his position. Forbidding. Angry. A barrier between Taryn and escape.

She zipped her suitcase shut and hefted it off the bed. Grabbing the matching overnight case from the floor, she moved his way. "I'm leaving. So you don't need to tell me to go."

She tried to edge past him, but he grabbed her arm in a tight hold. "You lied to me!"

Remorse bit into her soul. "Yes."

"Why?"

"I can't tell you."

"Did you help your brother murder your father?"

"Do you believe I could?"

A look of disgust on his face, he released her upper arm with an abrupt shake. "You're just as bad as Gwen was. And my mother. Evil. Self-seeking. Opportunistic. Everything you've said—everything you are—is a lie."

The words stung. But not as much as the wounded look in his eyes tore at her heart. She'd hurt him deeply. He had allowed himself to trust again, and she'd smothered that flicker of trust, probably killing his belief in any possible good in women once and for all.

"I'm so sorry, Dan," she whispered. "Believe me, there's nothing you can say that I haven't already told myself."

His eyes flickered, and for a moment she saw longing. Pain. Even love. Her heart wrenched as she swallowed the bitter taste of disappointment. They might have had such a nice life together. If only circumstances had been different.

"Please, let me go."

The cold look returned. "Why? So you can run again?" A muscle in his jaw jumped.

"It's all I can do."

"Then you must be guilty. If you weren't, you wouldn't run."

"In a sense I am guilty." Frustration made her clutch the suitcase handles more tightly. "But I can't talk about it now. Maybe never."

The distant wail of sirens sharpened her fear. "Please, Dan. Let me go!"

"If I did, I'd be guilty of aiding a criminal." His voice was gruff.

"If you don't, you'd be guilty of destroying me." She couldn't stop the tears from rolling. "I can't go back to California! Not now—not ever!"

She pushed against him hard, and he stumbled in surprise. Taking the opportunity, she wedged past. But he grabbed her arm before she could take more than a few hurried steps.

"You can't run forever, Taryn."

The name, foreign to his lips, grabbed her attention. She jerked her head up to look at his cheerless eyes and stony features.

"There's nothing else to do," she said hoarsely. Shaking her arm from his hold, she made her escape down the back stairs.

☙

Hours later, Taryn pulled her weary legs beneath her and opened another of her mother's letters. Laughter and loud music shook the thin plaster wall separating her from the motel's next room. A *thump* hit the wall, startling her. Someone was having a party, no doubt. Taryn's gaze went to the gold chain hanging from the door, and the bolt in its horizontal position. The phone didn't work, but at least the locks appeared to.

Assured that no wandering drunk could suddenly find his way inside her room, she returned her attention to the letter.

> *Tell me why it is, Mary, that no one warned us about being unequally yoked? Mother always wanted me to marry a good Catholic boy, but she neglected to warn me that I should never marry a man who didn't know God or go to church. I thought Charles did. He gave the impression he did. Still, I was desperate to leave the bad situation at home, to leave Ireland, and go to America. Even then, even had I known Charles was an atheist, I still might have married him. Is that horribly shocking? I was so miserable and foolish in my youth, and he always showered me with love and presents during those first years. I suppose I wasn't thinking clearly—but then, that is my trial. To act before thinking. I can see you shaking your head and smiling now, and it's glad I am that you've found such a good man in Sean. I wish you many happy years together.*
>
> *I'm so thankful that you've found Christ and am grateful my letters pointed you in that direction. Now we are truly sisters—remember how many times we wished it? I tell you, Mary, if I'd never met Hope and her husband at that movie opening, I might not have discovered the way to have a personal relationship with Jesus Christ, and I might not have*

had the strength to make it, what with Charles's constant drinking and surly behavior. We are wealthy—"filthy rich" some people call it. He's no longer a film assistant but an actual movie director for Hollywood. I won't tell you about the sin of this place; I think I already have. What saddens me is how far apart we've grown. He refuses to step foot inside a church, and lately he won't even talk to me. Yet I will continue on and accept the lot I've chosen. As Mother used to say, "You've made your bed; now you must lie in it." For the twins' sake, I will endure what I must.

Taryn's eyes misted at the loving remark made about her and Pat, and she brushed her finger over the blue looped words on the faded stationery.

Taryn and Patrick are my joy. They are six now, and already I see how Taryn takes Patrick under her wing, as if to protect him. She has such a mothering instinct. Patrick, on the other hand. . .well, he has a temper much like Charles's. The other day at the beach, a boy kicked sand on Patrick's Popsicle, and Patrick flew at him, punching him in the face. Of course, poor Taryn could hardly stand to see her brother get hit back—I couldn't, either, but I was too far away to do much good—and she jumped on the boy's back and pulled him off Patrick. She yelled at the boy then put her arm around her brother, whispering to him. He put his arm around her waist, and they walked off along the dunes together. They are always whispering to one another and have such a bond, one I some- times envy. I suppose that's what being a twin is like. I wish I would have had at least one brother or sister to play with and share secrets with—but at least I did have you.

And now I must tell you something, something I've told no one else, not even Charles. (He's filming on location in Spain.) I've been diagnosed with a serious disease—one of

those that has a long name I can't even spell—and must
undergo hospital treatments soon. . . .

A salty tear trickled to the corner of Taryn's mouth. She
wasn't sure she could keep reading, but neither could she stop.

If I shouldn't make it, dear Mary, can I have your promise
that you'll look after my children? Not financially, they'll have
more than enough money—but spiritually. My earnest prayer
is that the twins might come to know Christ as I have. And
while I'm on this earth, I will do all in my power to see that
happen. I'm so tired all the time and am not sure I have the
strength to fight this, on top of everything else. But I won't
give up, so don't worry. Perhaps, though, if the worst should
happen, you might send these letters to them when they're
grown, so they'll know how much their mother loved them. . . .

At this, Taryn fell prone on the bed and let the tears flow. . .
for her dear Irish mother, whose letters proved she had more
strength than she knew. . .for Patrick, her long-lost friend,
who'd become a frightening stranger when he started dab-
bling in drugs. . .for herself, at losing the people closest to her
heart. Her mother. Patrick. Dan.

Dear, wonderful Dan. He had tried so hard to trust her
despite all his just doubts. Her loss of him was the freshest
and hurt the most. How could she live without him, without
Paul and Gram and the cozy little inn on the other side of the
mountain, five hours away?

Feeling hollow, the well of her tears run dry, she made herself rise from the rumpled bedspread and wearily head for the
shower. Once she peeled off the velvet dress she'd bought for
the Christmas party, knowing Dan loved her in forest green,
she turned on the faucets and stepped inside. The water
scalded her skin, but it was no worse than the burning

remorse that ate away at her soul like acid.

Wrapped inside a towel, she stepped back into the main room. The sounds from next door had dimmed. Needing a distraction, Taryn clicked on the TV. Maybe she could lose herself in a movie, as she'd done repeatedly these past weeks.

She had just slipped into her flannel pajamas when her face flashed across the screen. In dread she turned up the volume and listened to the news reporter tell how she'd disappeared and was wanted for questioning. The reporter urged anyone with information to contact the toll-free number at the bottom of the screen.

Panic locked Taryn in a stranglehold. She'd left her glasses at the inn and had little disguise without them. The motel clerk had commented on what pretty hair she had. Hair like her mother's. Hair like the picture now plastered across the TV screen.

Fear spurring her into action, Taryn seized the nail scissors from her kit. Capturing a thick hank of her hair, she frantically sawed and cut at the damp chunk with the scissors. Her rapid breath came in whimpered gasps. Her teeth clenched in determination. Long auburn spirals came away in her hand.

She stared down at the shiny curls she clutched. Then her eyes turned upward to the destruction she'd wrought, and she realized what she'd done.

She was a destructive force—damaging herself. Damaging all those she loved. Her lies had dug her into a pit, a pit she had no idea how to escape. She was wanted by the police. Hunted. A criminal. . .

"Oh, God!" She threw the scissors at the mirror and sank to her knees, her forehead hitting the scarred dresser. "I can't go on! I'm scared, and I don't know where to run anymore! Help me!"

Like an ornament precariously dangling from a strand of garland, she might lose her hold at any moment. Plummet to the earth. Shatter. She leaned against the dresser, gulping back sobs. Trembling with fright. Feeling close to losing her sanity.

Memory of her mother's words drifted through her mind. Her mother had done what she had to do, even though it pained her, even though it wasn't easy. She hadn't given up. She hadn't chosen to hide in a corner when life got hard. She'd fought back. Strong. Courageous. Determined. A woman who knew how to brave her Goliath.

You can have what gave your mother strength, too. You just have to reach out and take it.

Taryn wasn't sure where the thought came from, but it quieted her. She did want it. Badly. But she didn't know how to take it. Or even what "it" was.

She stared at the water-stained rug. Minutes passed, but she didn't move. As she grew calmer, a strange confidence seeped into her being, and she rose from the threadbare carpet and slipped on her coat and shoes. Hiding her mangled hair in a scarf, she pocketed her motel key and a handful of quarters and set out to find a pay phone.

❧

"Paul, stop that racket!"

With wounded eyes, Paul looked up from wrapping a flat box in holly-sprigged paper. Dan instantly felt remorse.

"Sorry, buddy. Your old dad's just been on edge lately. What've you got there?" He tried to show interest.

"A picture I drew for Great-Grammy. I first made her a church nativity with some toothpicks I glued together, but it broke. So I drew her one with colored pencils instead. I drew a picture for Terri, too. Do you think she'll come back for Christmas?"

At the wistful words, Dan turned away from his son to look past the decorated tree to the overcast day outside. Overcast. Like his heart. "I don't think so, Paul. But I'm sure Great-Grammy will like the picture you drew for her."

"But I don't understand why Terri went away."

"She just had to go." Both he and Gram considered it best not to tell Paul about what happened. The boy had been in bed when Laura blew in with her shocking news and had slept through the entire thing. The small party was canceled and everyone had gone home.

Dan studied the snow-laden pines. He pictured romping through them and throwing snowballs with Terri and his son. Taryn, he mentally corrected. Taryn Rutherford. Wealthy socialite, and who knew what else. Not a struggling maid.

His initial anger and shock had diminished over the past four lonely days. Now all he felt was a dull ache in the center of his chest. He didn't want to celebrate Christmas, though for Paul he would go through the motions. Any joy over the holiday had left with Taryn. She'd had an impact on all their lives. On him.

Dan wasn't sure where the money was going to come from—he was in debt up to his eyeballs—but he'd made the difficult decision not to take the second job as a ski instructor. He wasn't going to spend any more time away from Paul, not when his son needed him so much. He'd talked to Pastor Trent two days ago and was surprised at how wise the young minister was. Dan felt an instant affinity for him and told him his troubles. The pastor listened then prayed with Dan, affirming that he was making the right choice and that his son was more important than taking the well-paying job. Soon the guests would start coming to rent rooms. Reservations had already been made. That was sure to boost finances.

Gram whisked into the room, a stack of colorful envelopes clutched in one hand. Paul grabbed his half-wrapped box to his chest and scrambled out the door.

"Something I did?" Gram's eyebrows lifted.

"He doesn't want his surprise spoiled."

"Oh, that's right. Christmas is tomorrow, isn't it?"

"Like you'd forgotten?" Dan countered with a grin.

Chuckling, she started to shuffle through the cards and study their addresses. "Oh, we got a card from the Robinsons this year! I'm not sure if I remembered to send them one. . . and here's one from the MacIntyres and the Braxtons. . . ."

Dan stared at the lush tree that Terri and Paul had worked so hard to decorate. The colored tinsel hung in perfect loops. First a row of green, then one of gold, then one of blue. . .

"You should call her."

"What?" He focused on his grandmother. "Who?"

"What do you mean, 'who'? Terri, of course."

"Gram, even if I wanted to call her, I have no idea where she is. Besides, why *should* I want to talk to her? You read the newspaper report."

"Oh, pish-posh. Terri is no more involved in conspiracy to commit murder than I am. Reporters speculate all the time." She continued flipping through the cards. "I'm sure she had a very good reason for leaving California as she did. She seems like such a nice girl, and in my morning times with the Lord, He never told me otherwise."

Dan blew out a resigned breath. It did no good to argue.

"Why, what's this?" Gram plucked a gold-embossed ivory envelope from the stack and set the rest down. "It's from an S. L. Sothby. Do you know an S. L. Sothby?"

"No. But you send and receive hundreds of Christmas cards every year. How can you expect to keep all the names straight?"

Gram was busily tearing into the envelope. She withdrew a card. Engraved on the front was a cheery hearth with a cozy fire. A cat and mouse snoozed on a braided rug underneath a row of hung stockings. The mouse lay nestled in the cat's fur, using the cat's tail for a cover. "Oh, isn't this just adorable!" She opened the card and something fluttered to the floor. She continued to stare at the inside of the card. "Why, that's odd.

It's signed, 'From a pleased guest.' There's no name."

Dan stooped to pick up the paper from the carpet and stared at it. Shock made his eyes go wide, and a sense of unreality hit him.

In his hands was a bank-certified check for twenty-five thousand dollars.

❧

On Christmas Eve, Taryn drove through the thickening dusk, hoping she wouldn't have to try to find the cabin in the dark. After locating a pay phone last night outside the rundown motel, she contacted her uncle. He was relieved to hear from her and promised not to tell anyone about her phone call—on one condition. That she come home for Christmas.

"I—I need more time," she'd sputtered. "I'll come home after New Year's, I promise."

"Pat's been worried about you," he scolded. "He asked me to call him the minute I heard anything."

"No!" Her uncle's admission chilled her soul. "I mean, I'd rather no one know yet."

"You two should talk," her uncle said gruffly. "He needs you."

"I can't—not yet." She sucked in a deep breath. "I, um, don't have enough money to tide me over for the next few weeks. Can you send some? I'll pay you back. I used most of what was in my wallet to get the motel room where I'm staying—in Colorado." She gave him the name of the town.

"That's about a half day's ride from where my cabin is. Why don't you stay there?" he added more quietly after a few seconds elapsed. "It's stocked with non-perishables, so you shouldn't starve."

Relief surged through Taryn at the offer. "Thanks, Uncle Matt. I will."

She'd gotten directions and, after assuring him that she would return home soon, hung up the phone. Now she continued to drive down the winding road, past occasional buildings and homes decked out in glowing Christmas finery. She spotted a gas station on the left, recognized the name on the sign from her uncle's directions, and turned right at the next street. Her thoughts skittered to her brother. The idea of betraying her twin was hard. She was sure she would be forced to testify. And that meant telling the truth, the truth that only she and Pat knew.

Patrick had murdered their father in cold blood. Taryn saw him. And what's more, he'd seen her near the trees once he lowered the shotgun.

Taryn withheld a shiver and flicked the car's heater up a notch. The sky was now a canopy of inky blue-blackness. Her headlights caught a deer, and she eased on the brake, thankful she was going well under the speed limit and hadn't struck it. The graceful doe looked at her then loped into the thick woods. Taryn slowly accelerated, paying close attention to the landscape as she hunted for the narrow lane leading to the cabin.

At last she spotted the turnoff. The rutted road was narrow. Tall, massive trees gave the impression of closing in on her. Just ahead, she could see her uncle's log cabin. Its curtained windows were flooded with yellow light, and a plume of smoke curled from the chimney.

That was odd. Or maybe not. Uncle Matt must have called a neighbor to ready the place for her. She only hoped he had neglected to reveal the identity of his visitor. She wasn't ready for her whereabouts to be known by anyone. Even a stranger in a remote mountain town.

Her tires scrunched over the slushy U-drive, and she parked the car. Weary, she grabbed her luggage from the back seat and headed up the walk. Her eyes searched the ground for the round gray rocklike safe that held the concealed cabin key.

The door swung inward, and she glanced up. Her heart froze to a solid lump. The glaring porch light exposed the features of the man who blocked her entrance.

Patrick!

Her suitcases crashed to the ground. Shaking her head, she backed away. Spun on her heel. Ran for her life. Past the car. To the safety of the thick trees.

A strong hand seized her arm. Yanked her around.

She screamed loud and long—then raised her arm to block Patrick's hand swinging down to her face.

twelve

"Taryn—stop it!"

The sting of his slap stifled her hysterical screams. She sucked in gasping gulps of air as if she'd been drowning. Lifting a shaky hand to her red-hot cheek, she stared at him, her eyes brimming with tears.

He grabbed her other arm and shook her slightly. "What's gotten into you?"

"You should know the answer to that!"

He hissed out a breath, releasing her. "We need to talk." His voice was low.

"I don't want to talk!"

"Then why did you come?"

"Well, I sure didn't know *you* would be here!"

Surprise etched his features. "Uncle Matt didn't tell you? He phoned this morning to tell me you were on the way."

Betrayed by her own uncle! Taryn briskly rubbed her coat sleeves, wondering if she dared attempt another getaway. As though sensing her intentions, Patrick again grabbed her arm.

"Come on. You'll freeze to death out here. Let's talk inside where it's warm."

She tried to break loose, but his hold was firm. "I told you. I don't want to talk to you." Suddenly she noticed another figure standing in the doorway. Her cousin Luke. "Why's Luke here?"

"He's staying with me. I found it necessary to hide out from the media and curiosity seekers."

That she could understand. Taryn allowed Patrick to lead her into the cabin. With her cousin there, surely she would be safe.

Luke hugged her. "It's good to see you again, Taryn. Come on inside. I'll put your luggage in the spare room. Oh—you dropped this." He pushed her purse into her hand. Automatically she clutched it and brought it to her chest.

"If you two need me for anything, holler," Luke said. "I'll be in the kitchen making some coffee."

Taryn could only nod. Patrick motioned to the next room. Two brown sofas formed an L in the sunken den. One of her uncle's hunting trophies hung from the paneled walls. She avoided looking at the glassy eyes of the poor creature—shot, stuffed, its head exhibited for display. She abhorred her family's desire to hunt whatever happened to be in season. Walking stiffly over the polished wooden floor, she jammed her hands deep into her pockets, took a seat on one of the sofas, and stared straight ahead. The couch shifted as Patrick sank to the cushion beside hers and clasped his hands between his knees. She managed not to flee to the other sofa. Tense seconds crackled by like the fire in the grate.

"Maybe you'd better tell me what happened out there," Patrick said at last. "Why'd you run from me?"

"How can you even ask that?" Taryn shot back bitterly. "I saw what you did to our father."

"I'm not sure what you think you saw, but you'd better tell me."

"No." She shivered despite the warm room. "I'd rather forget that night."

"You can't, Taryn. None of us can. And it won't be over for a long time. So just tell me what you saw."

His voice sounded dead, emotionless. Taryn turned her head to look at him. His jaw was taut, and moisture skimmed his blue-green eyes as he stared into the fire.

She looked back at the flames. Tightness clogged her throat, making it difficult to speak. Still, she skirted the issue, wanting to put off speaking of that horrible moment for as long as she could. "I had a blind date that night—a favor to a friend—Lisa. But the guy was a jerk. After we had dinner, he drove me to the park not far from our house and was all over me within seconds. I told him to stop. When he didn't, I kneed him in the groin, pushed him off me, and slammed the door in his face. Then I walked home. Thankfully, he didn't come after me, though I saw his car race past when I hit the main road."

She didn't look at Patrick though she could sense his tension.

"I took a shortcut through the woods by our house," she continued. "I was trying to hurry home, because it was almost dark and I didn't want that guy to find me if he changed his mind and came back looking. That's when I heard the shot." She swallowed and forced herself to go on. "I reached the clearing and saw you standing there with the shotgun. And I saw him lying on the leaves. You just stood there—then you looked my way. I panicked and ran."

Thick silence smothered Taryn. She fought to steady her breathing.

"I stumbled," Patrick said.

"What?" She turned her head sharply to look at him.

"I stumbled." His sad gaze met hers. "I was upset—he yelled at me for scaring the ducks with my crazy shot when I tried to bag one. Taryn, we shouldn't even have been hunting. There were three weeks left until the season started, but you know our father. He argued that he should be allowed to do what he wanted on his own land, and. . ." He looked away, as if ashamed. "And I was coming down off a high. The shotgun's safety wasn't on. He kept yelling at me, telling me what a loser I was. Then he walked ahead of me. I wasn't watching where I was going. I tripped over a stump, and the gun went off."

"The news report said the maid heard you fighting."

"We were. I'd been gone for two days with my friends, and when I came home, Father was walking out the door. He ordered me to grab my shotgun and join him. But, Taryn, I didn't mean to kill him. I've thought it at times, sure, like when he would give me a bloody lip or a black eye. But I never meant to kill him. Maybe I'm paying for all those bad thoughts I had. I don't know. But the thought never crossed my mind that night. I was too busy feeling sorry for myself."

Taryn mulled over his words. A number of times their father had taken his anger out on Patrick. Taryn had never been hit, but she'd been wounded by the man's words, which inflicted their own brand of pain. There were even times when his vicious taunts and cruel remarks hurt her so deeply she also wished him dead, and for that she felt doubly sorry now.

Patrick straightened from his hunched position. "The case is going to trial early next summer. At the preliminary hearing, I refused to plea bargain for the lesser charge of voluntary manslaughter and three years' jail time—all the district attorney would agree to—because I didn't voluntarily kill anyone. Whatever happens, I need you to believe that."

"I want to. You don't know how desperately I want to," Taryn said under her breath.

Patrick closed his eyes in resignation. "I understand. After the way I've acted all these years, how can you believe me? And who could blame you?" He raked his fingers through his hair, clutching it tightly at the back, before dropping his hands between his knees again. "There've been times I even wondered if I shouldn't just go ahead and plea bargain and take what they give me. Anything would be better than being convicted of first-degree murder."

"What stopped you?"

"Uncle Matt. He told me that he'd get the best lawyer money could buy. And I felt that if Father's brother was on my side, then at least he must believe me."

She lowered her gaze to her lap. "I'm sorry I wasn't there for you, Pat. This is the first time I've ever deserted you. I just didn't know what to think."

"Like I said, I understand." He cleared his throat, seeming suddenly nervous. "There's something else I need to tell you, Taryn. Before Uncle Matt bailed me out of jail, I was scared stiff. I'd never been in a place like that before. I'm still scared, but not like I was. Alone with Luke in the cabin these past weeks. . .well, he's helped me find some peace." His expression grew softer. "I've become a believer in Jesus Christ. I know I may go to prison, but I've come to a place where I can deal with that now. Because I know God'll take care of me. Even there."

Taryn stared openmouthed.

Patrick chuckled dryly. "You're floored. I don't blame you. But apparently God wants even the reprobates. Luke showed me a few examples of bad-guys-turned-good in the Bible. Paul—the guy who wrote a lot of the New Testament—was a murderer. Did you know that?"

Wordlessly, Taryn shook her head.

"Abraham and Peter were liars—or at least they lied when things got bad—and the list goes on. Our cuz did quite a bit of talking during our time here, but he finally convinced me. And, Taryn, no matter what happens with the trial, I know that God's going to help me deal with it, because He's at the wheel of my life now."

Hot moisture coated her eyes. Pain tightened her throat. She reached into her purse for the letters. "Here," she said, tossing them onto Patrick's lap. "You'll want to read those."

Patrick lifted his brow at her lightning-quick change in topic. He pulled one of the letters from the packet, sucking in a loud breath when he saw the return address. "From our mother? How'd you get these?"

"An inn where I was staying—there was a cook there. I'll tell you all about it later. Just read."

Taryn watched as he carefully smoothed out the rose-colored

stationery on his jeans leg and began reading. After a time, he opened another letter. Then another. Finally he turned to her, his eyes glistening.

"This is unbelievable. All along she was praying for us to find Christ."

Taryn gave a slight nod. "Is it hard?"

"Is what hard?"

"Becoming a Christian. I—I've thought about it a lot these past weeks, but I've been scared that God wouldn't want me because of what I'd done."

"What did you do?" He looked puzzled.

"I pretended to be someone I wasn't. I lied to a very special man and his family and hurt them without intending to. I deceived people—and ran from the police. I was afraid they would force me to testify against you."

His hand slipped over hers. The warmth of his touch now reassured instead of frightened. "Taryn, according to Luke, there's nothing you can do while you're on this earth that God can't forgive. But you've got to stop running." His other hand went to her short chunk of hair, and he fingered the choppy ends. "No offense, but you look awful. What happened?"

She shrugged. "I panicked when I saw my picture on the news and cut it off before I could think about what I was doing."

"Oh, man, Taryn. I don't want you taking this out on yourself anymore. You've got to stop running. If you're forced to testify, so be it. We'll talk to my lawyer, get his advice, and deal with it when the time comes." Pain filled his eyes. "I'm going to get help. For my drug dependency. I've been dried out since that night, but it's been hard. Even after all that's happened, I find myself wanting a snort now and then."

"I'll help you any way I can," she said, meaning every word. "I feel like I've let you down."

"No," he interrupted quietly. "I let myself down. You've

always been a rock of support." He squeezed her hand.

Emotion made her swallow. She could hardly believe this was her brother talking. "Patrick, I really do want to become a Christian. But I don't know how or what to say. Will you help me?"

"Just say what's in your heart. That's what Luke had me do. Tell Jesus you're sorry for your sins, that you believe He's God, and that you want Him in control of your life."

Taryn nodded and bowed her head. "Dear Lord," she murmured. "I've blown it in so many ways, I'm not even sure I can remember all of them. I lied, I was cruel to Dan, and I evaded the law. Please forgive me for all of it. I believe that You're God and that You died and rose again, as Gram said. And I do want You to take control of my life. Jesus, I accept You as my Lord," she added, remembering something she'd heard at Gram's church during the altar call. She'd been standing in the foyer, near the door, terrified of the pastor's message; but she'd heard bits and pieces of the prayer.

Taryn inhaled deeply, smelling the rich coffee percolating in the next room. She felt lighter, her senses sharply in tune.

"And, Lord, please prepare my sister—prepare us both—for whatever lies ahead," Patrick added somewhat awkwardly. "Give us the strength to go on and face whatever we have to."

Taryn looked up. Patrick's eyes were shining.

"Do you think Mama knows?" she whispered.

Patrick smiled and nodded. They hugged one another tightly.

&

Gentle strains of instrumental Christmas hymns from an old-fashioned cabinet stereo drifted through the cabin. Luke was on the phone in the next room, talking to his family. Patrick's lanky form lay stretched out on one of the two sofas in the den. Shaking her head, Taryn smiled and picked up the thick quilt he'd kicked off in his sleep. When they were children

and took naps together, he always kicked off all the covers
and she woke up cold.

She covered him, tucking the folds around his flannel shirt
and smoothed his long, wavy brown locks from his closed eyes.
In sleep, he appeared so much like a little boy. So innocent; so
peaceful.

She softly exhaled and straightened. By his words and
actions last night and today, she now believed his story. But
would a jury? Or would her testimony hurt Patrick?

Taryn prepared a mug of coffee, diluting it with milk and
sugar. She added a peppermint stick in honor of the holiday,
wishing for her own Irish mint cappuccino. Meditative, she
stirred the coffee.

Christmas Day. She had planned to spend it so much differently, but at least she was with her family. And she was
now a member of God's family, too. She still felt a little in
awe that He would even want her. Picking up one of her
mother's letters lying open on the counter, she studied the
familiar words that she'd soaked up many times that morning.

*I may not know what the future holds, dear Mary, but one
thing I do know. No matter what trials I encounter, no matter what storms I face, I've learned that to run straight into
the arms of Jesus is the only way to survive. He will hold me
and keep me safe. . . .*

The awe-inspiring words from almost two decades ago
reached out to Taryn, reassuring her. Strengthening her. At
this point, she was sure she could make it through the next
months. And it was time to do something else, too.

Finding a clean sheet of paper and an envelope, she began:

Dear Dan,
*   After what I've done to you and your family, asking for*

forgiveness seems almost laughable right now. Yet I'm hoping you can find it in your heart not to judge me too harshly. Before I left Pinecrest, you asked me why I lied about who I was. I couldn't tell you then, but now I can. I want to tell you the truth. I need to.

In hiding myself, as I did all those weeks at your inn, I shielded my brother Patrick. I was scared of him and of everything connected to the case. But at the same time, I didn't want to see him go to prison for killing our father. The news report was right when it said that I fled from the scene of the crime. I saw the whole thing—or I thought I did anyway—though I took no part in it. Since talking to Patrick, I realize now that I saw only a portion of what happened. After the shooting, I ran to the house, grabbed my car keys, and tossed a few things into a suitcase without really being aware of what I was doing. Then I fled. My actions and reasoning are probably incomprehensible to you—I was more than a little upset and in a state of shock, and I acted without thinking things through. Above all, I loved Patrick and wanted to protect him—I still love him, though I know I can't shield him from this. And that frustrates me so much. We were born three minutes apart, but I've always felt like I was older than him by years, not minutes.

Before I draw this letter to a close, I must tell you something that's happened to me—something I want you to tell Gram. I've accepted Jesus as my Savior through my own brother's counsel—Patrick has become a Christian, too! And for the first time I feel at peace, though nothing is resolved concerning the case. It goes to trial in May. Please tell Mary it was through my mother's letters that I found the courage I needed to stop running, and thank her for me. Tell Paul that I'm sorry I had to go without saying good-bye and that I enjoyed our time together. He's a wonderful little boy. As for you, Dan, I can only say that I'm truly sorry. The last three weeks *we spent together were undoubtedly the happiest I've had in a long time. Thank you for that and for allowing me to be part of your family for the short time I was. It was a gift I shall always cherish. I pray that you, too, might find peace one day.*

Taryn stuck the bottom end of the ballpoint pen to her mouth, wanting to say so much more. Wanting to tell him how much she loved him. Wanting to beg him to forgive her and allow her to come back to Pinecrest at some point in the future. She skimmed the page and frowned. Perhaps she'd said too much already. With a continuous row of curlicues, she crossed out everything that came after her apology, though she kept in the part about wanting him to find peace. She signed it, "God bless you this Christmas and always, Taryn Rutherford." Satisfied that she'd done what she could to make amends, she readied an envelope and located a stamp. She surveyed the words once more before folding the letter twice.

Dan probably had received the anonymous card and check by now. At least she hoped he had. The gesture didn't completely assuage her guilt, but it did ease her conscience to know that she'd helped to lift Dan's worries over money. Something she had in abundant supply—when she could get to it without fear of being traced. Until then, her uncle had assured her over the motel's pay phone that he'd take care of the matter for her. He'd told her of his plan to write a check to a good friend and have this friend go to the bank and get a cashier's check from his own account. That way Dan wouldn't be tipped off, since the name Rutherford was plastered all over the news. Uncle Matt briefly had questioned her about just who Dan was to her, and likely had heard the truth behind her faltering replies.

Taryn looked out the window at the still, white wonderland. It had stopped snowing an hour ago, and last night she'd spotted a blue mailbox near the minimart, which was only half a mile or so down the road. Deciding she would rather walk than drive, she slid the letter into her coat pocket, jotted a note to Patrick and Luke, and let herself outdoors.

The air was crisp, the walk reviving. She felt strangely buoyant as she crunched through the snow, and her breath misted the air. Traffic was scarce, the holiday keeping everyone indoors. Soon she arrived at the closed store, slipped her letter into the mailbox at the road's edge, and retraced her steps to the cabin.

How different this Christmas had turned out from Christmases past! At home, she'd known only warm and balmy holidays. For the first time she was experiencing a white Christmas—and loved it. She looked forward to snowball fights and snowmen construction. Today, there were no wrapped boxes waiting for her beneath a Scotch pine. Yet she'd received two of the best gifts. Reconciliation with her brother, and the knowledge that she belonged to a God who loved her. Her mother's letters were also a wonderful present. If only she could receive the gift of Dan's forgiveness, her holiday would be complete.

Catching sight of Patrick's face at the window, Taryn smiled and waved to him as she came up the drive. She didn't know what the future held. But for this one day she vowed to forget whatever fearsome obstacles might lie in wait and enjoy the present—God's gift to them both. Just for today, she and her brother would be children again.

thirteen

The morning sun blinded Taryn's unprotected eyes as she was rushed past the media and up the stairs of the criminal courts building. A familiar face caught her attention. Dan?

Shocked, she swung her head to the side to search the blur of faces. No, he wasn't there. She must have just seen someone who looked like him.

Patrick's lawyer continued to pull her up the stairs, and she turned her concentration to the cement steps again. Her brother hurried up the other side, ignoring the barrage of questions and news microphones shoved in his face. They had tried using another entrance to slip by unnoticed, but the media had found them.

Outside the paneled courtroom doors, Taryn put her hand to the sleeve of Patrick's suit. Today she would be called as a witness. They'd said everything that needed to be said earlier. It was a good thing, because no words would come now. She hoped her eyes conveyed what she wanted to tell him. That she loved him; that she was there for him. And that no matter what the prosecution did to her on the witness stand, she believed in him. Patrick tipped his head, the barest hint of a smile on his rigid face. The gentle look in his eyes told her that he understood, that no matter what happened, they would make it through this and be all right. Taryn felt relieved that the bond they'd always shared as twins hadn't been destroyed. Once again they could read each other.

Mr. Phelps, Patrick's lawyer, entered the courtroom with her brother while Taryn was escorted to another room where she would wait until they called her. Sports and ladies' fashion magazines littered the table in front of the sofa, but Taryn couldn't think about reading. Instead, she took a seat and mulled over the last several months.

When she'd returned to her uncle's home after her brief holiday interlude with Patrick, the police came, and she was taken in for questioning. Later she was charged with conspiracy—during the investigation, they'd found her triangular coat button at the scene of the crime—but the charge against her was soon dropped due to insufficient evidence. Patrick's lawyer cautioned her that because her testimony was harmful to Patrick, the district attorney would undoubtedly subpoena her, and he had. Mr. Phelps also told her of his plan to try to discredit her on the stand. After all, she'd been upset that night due to the near date rape.

In the weeks that followed, he and his assistant worked with both her and Patrick. They asked harsh questions—questions the prosecution might ask. Afterward, Mr. Phelps advised Patrick not to take the witness stand. Patrick angered too easily, especially when Mr. Phelps's probing questions made Taryn cry. And that could work against him if he exhibited such an outburst during a cross-examination. It was all up to Taryn now. Only her testimony could save her brother.

She shivered, though the room temperature was moderate. "How, Lord, how can I do this?"

Rest in Me.

The quiet, reassuring thought filled an empty crevice in her spirit, and she relaxed her head back against the black vinyl cushion. Somehow God would give her what she needed to brave her Goliath.

Soon the door opened and a bailiff came for her. Swallowing hard, she stood, smoothed the wrinkles from her skirt, and followed the uniformed man into the packed courtroom. On trembling legs she walked down the center aisle, past the swinging door of the wooden bar railing, and up to the witness stand. She was sworn in. Told to be seated.

Cupping her palms face-up in her lap, she tried to relax. Remember all of Mr. Phelps's instructions to her. Phrase her answers carefully.

As the prosecutor approached, the look in his deep-set blue eyes reminded her of the predator zeroing in for the kill.

"Miss Rutherford, in your statement you said that you came to the clearing and it was then that you saw your brother holding the shotgun. Is that correct?"

"Yes, sir."

"How far away was he standing from you?"

"I don't recall."

"If you could give an estimate, say, were you within twenty to thirty feet of him?"

Taryn thought a moment. "Yes, sir."

"What about ten to twenty feet?"

"I'm not sure."

The prosecutor walked around to his long table and picked up a colored blown-up picture of the wooded area and the clearing. "I again bring before the court exhibit thirty-five. I will remind the jury that this is a picture of the crime scene taken on the morning after the shooting. Miss Rutherford, would you please point out where you stood when you first saw your brother."

She studied the picture and jabbed a shaky finger near a maple tree at the clearing's edge.

"And now if you could point to where your brother was standing."

She motioned to a patch of brown grass in the clearing.

"Thank you." He held the placard up. "Let the records show that, according to the testimony of expert witness Sheriff Monohan, the witness pointed out an area with no more than ten feet between her and the defendant." He gave the placard to a clerk and looked at Taryn again. "When you first saw your brother, how was he holding the gun?"

"He had it cradled under one arm, sort of just hanging there."

The prosecutor walked toward her. "Did he make any effort to go to your father?"

Taryn swallowed. "No, sir."

"What exactly did your brother do?"

"He, um, just stood there looking at him."

"Would you describe your brother as acting upset?"

"I'm not sure."

"You're not sure?"

"He didn't do much of anything. He acted like he was in shock."

"Did he see you?"

"I–I think so."

"You think so," the prosecutor repeated. "Did he turn his head your way or give any outward indication that he'd spotted you?"

"He looked my way." Taryn began twisting her ring. "But it was getting dark, and I couldn't tell if he'd seen me or not."

"If that's true, then why did you run?"

"Objection," Mr. Phelps stated. "Argumentative."

"I'll rephrase," the prosecutor said. "What did you do after you thought your brother might have seen you?"

"I ran to the house."

"Did he call out to you?"

Taryn pulled her ring past the first knuckle then shoved it back down. "Yes."

"Why didn't you answer?"

"I–I wasn't thinking clearly."

"And what happened then?"

"I fell and got up—then kept running. But I was in shock—"

"What did you do when you reached the house?" he asked, cutting her off.

"I. . .I packed my bags and left."

"Did you call 911 first?"

"No," she whispered. "Juanita—the maid was doing it."

"Did you tell the maid to call 911?"

"Yes, sir."

"And what were your exact words to her at the time?"

"I"—she targeted a look at Patrick, her heart sinking—"I told her that Patrick shot Father and to call for help."

"Those were your exact words?"

"I think so. I can't recall for sure."

He paced away from the witness box then faced her again. "In your statement, you stated that you were upset and that's why you disappeared after the shooting. Is that correct?"

"Yes, sir."

"But surely, if you thought the shooting an accident as you earlier stated, you would have had no reason to flee to another state."

"I was confused."

"Confused." He moved closer, his thick, black brows lifted. "Your father lay bleeding to death on the grass, your brother stood over him with a smoking shotgun—and you were confused."

"Objection, Your Honor," Mr. Phelps cut in. "Is this a question?"

"Sustained. Jury will disregard the last remark." The judge frowned. "If you're making a point, Counselor, please get to it."

"Thank you, Your Honor. I intend to." The prosecutor, Mr. Carstairs, moved toward his table and picked up a packet. "Such actions on your part suggest more than mere confusion, Miss Rutherford. In the deposition on page six, would you please silently read the third paragraph?"

She did so then handed the packet back to him, her heart sinking lower.

"On the statement that you gave the police you mentioned that you were frightened and that's why you left town. Is that correct?"

"Yes, sir."

"Were you frightened of your brother?"

"A little," Taryn answered quietly, looking at Patrick in apology.

Mr. Carstairs cupped a hand behind his ear. "Excuse me? I can't hear you. Could you please speak into the microphone?"

"A little," she said, bending toward the mouthpiece.

"A little. And so by your own admission, you've stated that you were afraid of your brother on the night that your father was murdered. Is that correct?"

"Objection!" Mr. Phelps bellowed. "I ask that the remark be stricken from the record. We have yet to determine whether Charles Rutherford was murdered or not."

The judge nodded and ordered the court reporter to do so.

"Was your brother abusive toward you, Miss Rutherford?" the prosecutor asked.

"Abusive?" She thought about his many acidic words to her in the past five years. "Not physically, no."

"No?" He sounded amazed. "Yet isn't it true that his violent behavior put that scar on your face?"

Shocked to realize he knew about that, too, Taryn instinctively brought her icy fingers to her cheekbone even as Mr. Phelps called out another objection. "Relevance!" he argued.

"Your Honor," Mr. Carstairs told the judge, "my question is very relevant to this case in that it's meant to reveal a history of the defendant's sudden and violent outbursts toward his family members, the witness included."

The judge considered, then nodded. "Overruled."

"Thank you, Your Honor," the prosecutor said.

The judge looked at Taryn. "Answer the question."

Taryn swallowed. "It was an accident." She directed her

reply to the judge, whose words to her had seemed softer than the prosecutor's.

"Just answer yes or no, Miss Rutherford, did your brother's violent behavior put that scar on your face?" Mr. Carstairs moved closer.

"We were arguing"—tears sprang to Taryn's eyes—"and he pushed me. I lost my balance and fell on a broken vase—"

"Yes or no, Miss Rutherford!"

She swung her head around. "Yes, but it wasn't all his fault—"

The prosecutor leaned in toward her. "And isn't it also true that you left town on the night your father was killed because you were afraid your brother would harm you again?" He ignored her last remark and continued without missing a beat. "That you remained missing for three months—because you saw your brother shoot your father down in cold blood and were afraid he'd do the same thing to you?"

"I—no—I—"

"Objection!" Mr. Phelps threw down his pencil on the pad on which he'd been scribbling notes and shot out of his chair. "Your Honor, may we approach the bench?"

"That would be wise." The judge's voice held a hint of impatience, and she banged her gavel to silence the buzzing voices in the courtroom. "I will have order in this court!"

The room quieted. Taryn only half-heard the judge and two lawyers confer in lowered tones. She hazarded a glance toward the seven women and five men of the jury seated near her. From the blank looks on their faces, it was difficult to tell what they thought. Her gaze moved past Patrick, who was staring down at his clasped hands on the table, then to the people behind the railing, observing the trial. Suddenly her breath caught in her throat, and her eyes widened.

Next to Uncle Matt, in the front row, sat Dan Carr. And he was looking straight at her.

❧

Dan forced what he hoped was an encouraging expression to his face, trying to bolster her courage. He still couldn't get over the change in Taryn since he'd last seen her. Her hair was chopped jaw-length, now resembling a corkscrew mop of reddish brown curls, and she'd lost too much weight. Her clothes hung on her. She looked so fragile up there, sitting all alone, and Dan had to restrain himself from walking past the bar and taking her in his arms. Her face was too pale, the bloom in her cheeks that she'd regained at the inn, missing.

He hoped the judge was giving the prosecuting attorney an earful. A few times during the line of questioning, when he watched the D.A. smoothly rip her into mincemeat, Dan could have wrung the man's neck. He wanted to protest that she was the victim, not the villain, but of course he could do nothing.

Two nights before he received her apology letter, he'd forgiven her. Frustrated, he'd held that paper up to the light, trying to decipher what she'd scratched out with the rows of loops, and finally made out the sweet words. His heart leaped when he saw that she must love him, despite his dreadful behavior toward her at the inn. He was also amazed that she'd accepted Christ on Christmas Eve, the same day he made the decision to turn his life over to the Lord.

After finally hunting down S. L. Sothby, the name on the check, Dan convinced the man to give him her uncle's number. It hadn't taken him long to realize the twenty-five thousand dollars must be from Taryn and that she had engineered the anonymous donor "guest" so Dan wouldn't suspect. At first he warred with pride and wouldn't deposit the check. But after Gram's gentle admonition, Dan realized he couldn't refuse the gift, not when they needed it so badly to keep the inn.

The lawyers moved away from the judge's high desk. The

prosecutor asked a few more questions then ended his examination. The judge asked the defense if he wished to cross-examine, and he agreed. Quietly Taryn answered his questions. This time she seemed in better control of herself. Yes, it was getting dark that night; it was possible that she might not have seen things clearly. She was still upset because of the near date rape. She'd walked more than a mile in high heels and was a little frightened that the guy might change his mind and come after her. That's why she'd taken the shortcut through the woods. No, she didn't see Patrick actually shoot the gun. She came to the clearing after the shot was fired. Based on the little she saw, it could have been a careless accident.

When Taryn was dismissed from the witness stand, the judge hit her gavel. "Court will recess for lunch and reconvene in one hour."

Dan stood, intending to make a beeline for the courtroom doors, but Matt's hand touched his shoulder.

"You won't find her out there, in that pack of wolves," he said. "Come with me. I'll take you to her."

Dan exited the courtroom with Matt, who stood almost as tall as he. A few reporters tried to get Taryn's uncle to answer questions, but he just shook his graying head and swept past them. Dan was beginning to understand why Taryn had spent months avoiding the media. Matt led him outside to the rear of the building, and a white Cadillac rolled to a stop beside the two men. Matt opened the back door.

"Get in. I'll meet you at the house."

Dan hunched over to slide inside—and spotted Taryn sitting by the opposite door. Her gray eyes widened in surprise. The car pulled away from the courthouse.

"You came." Her words were soft, trembling. The strain on her chalky face called every protective gene Dan possessed into action, and he twisted on the seat to hold his arm out to her as an invitation.

"I came," he acknowledged.

With a little sob, Taryn closed the distance between them and buried herself in his embrace. "I hurt him, Dan! I hurt Pat. My testimony will send him to prison for sure."

Dan didn't know enough about the brother or the case to determine his innocence or guilt. The trial had been going on for a week, but Dan had only arrived in California today. His one desire now was to comfort. "You don't know that. It's up to the jury to decide. They didn't look as if they disbelieved you."

"But they didn't look as if they believed me, either. In fact, they didn't have any kind of expression on their faces. They would make great poker players."

He smiled at her attempted joke.

"I'm so glad you came," she murmured into the shoulder of his suit coat. "I didn't think I'd ever see you again."

Her admission brought back memory of his cruel words that last day at the inn, and he winced. He focused on the line of stately palm trees etched against a cloudless blue sky as the car drove past them.

"Terri, er, Taryn. . ."

"You can call me Terri if you want to."

"Okay. Since I got your letter, I've done everything possible to find you. I was angry that night, but I never should have said what I did."

"You had every right to say those things. I lied to you."

"Yes, but your reasons weren't selfish ones. In your own desperate way, you were trying to be loyal to your brother and protect both of you. I see that now."

She lifted her head to look at him and moved out of his arms. "If what I did wasn't wrong, then why did I feel so bad about tricking everyone into thinking I was someone else?"

"I'm not saying your actions weren't wrong. Only that I was just as wrong to lash out at you like I did. I want you to know how sorry I am. I've spent some time counseling with Pastor

Trent, and I see a lot of things differently now."

"Counseling?"

"I accepted Christ the same day you did. On Christmas Eve."

"Really?" Her eyes grew round.

He chuckled. "Yes, really. I also figured out those sentences you scribbled through in your letter. You should never do that to a person, Terri. Curiosity just about ate me away, and I almost got eyestrain. But it was worth it."

Her cheeks glowed. It was good to see color come back to her face again. "You read all that?"

"Yes. If I hadn't, I might not have come."

"But you did come."

"Yes." He saw the question in her eyes. "Because I feel the same way. Those last weeks with you were some of the best weeks I've had in a while. You opened my eyes to a lot of things, and when I read in your letter that you cared about me, too, I had to find you." He slid his hand into hers and interlaced their fingers. "I want you to come back with me to Pinecrest."

Surprise softened her face. "Dan, I can't. Not with the trial—"

He nodded. "Of course you can't right now. I know that. I meant after a verdict is reached."

"Can you stay that long? This trial could go on for several more weeks, even months."

"I'll stay as long as you need me to. My cousin doesn't have a job right now. The airline she was flying for went bankrupt, and she's working at the inn. Gram is doing better these days, so I can take the time away." He cleared his throat nervously. "I know you can't think of the future past this trial, but I want to make something abundantly clear. I wasn't just asking you to come back with me as a guest, so that you could get away from any post-trial trauma. I want to take you back to Pinecrest as my fiancée, or better yet, my wife."

Shock widened her eyes. "Dan—"

"I know. My timing's lousy, but in the past when I held back what I wanted to say, I regretted it later. Just think about it, Terri. You don't have to make a decision right now. I don't expect you to."

She nodded, and he slid his other arm around her. Tilting her head against his shoulder, she closed her eyes. He studied her profile, noting the faint worry lines in her forehead that hadn't been there months ago.

"I promise to do all I can to help you through the coming days," he whispered. With his thumb, he stroked her hand still clasped in his. "Even if that means only being there as a support to rest against when you get weary, I'll be there for you."

Her other arm snaked across his chest, and she hugged him tightly. "I'm counting on it, Dan. I need all the support I can get."

੨ə

After nine more weeks, a total of forty-two witnesses, including a few celebrities, and numerous visual exhibits and pieces of evidence, the prosecution and defense made their closing statements, and the jury was dismissed to make a decision. Now, three and a half days later, the men and women of the jury returned to their box.

Taryn watched them file in, her heart beating fast. Dan sat beside her, his arm tight around her waist.

"Has the jury reached a verdict?" the judge asked.

"We have, Your Honor." The foreman handed a slip of folded paper to the clerk, who took it to the judge. The judge opened it, read it, then handed it back to the clerk. Taryn thought she might go insane with the wait. She directed a look toward Patrick.

He sat tall and didn't falter. Earlier this morning he'd told her about the strange dream he'd had last night. In it he had walked a gloomy, overgrown path, one he wouldn't have chosen. But suddenly a bearded man in a long tunic was walking beside him. Then he woke up.

"Will the clerk please read the verdict," the judge ordered.

The balding man adjusted his glasses and cleared his throat. "Superior Court of California, County of Los Angeles, in the matter of the State of California versus Patrick Rutherford, case number BA 598221. We the jury, in the above-entitled action, find the defendant, Patrick Rutherford, *not guilty* of the crime of first-degree murder. Same title, same cause. We the jury in the above-entitled action, find the defendant, Patrick Rutherford, *guilty* of voluntary manslaughter. . . ."

The courtroom erupted, the judge banged her gavel, and Taryn felt her world spin. Dan's iron-muscled arm was all that held her up as the clerk continued reading.

"Ladies and gentlemen of the jury, were these and are these your verdicts as read?" the clerk asked.

The foreman stood up and nodded once. "Yes, sir."

Heartbroken, Taryn glanced at Patrick. He swung his gaze in her direction. His expression was calm, sober, accepting, as if he'd known he was going to prison all along. A bailiff approached to take her brother away.

"Shall we have the jury polled?" the judge asked.

"No, thank you," both lawyers responded.

"Record the verdicts, please."

Taryn barely grasped the rest of the proceedings as the judge scheduled sentencing for the following morning, addressed the jury, and then dismissed the court.

"Come on," Dan said, pulling her to her feet. "Let's get you out of here."

"But Patrick—" she argued, her voice not sounding like her own. She watched her uncle move forward to hug her brother.

"You can visit him later. Right now we need to get you home."

Dan steered her out of the crowded courtroom, down the

corridor, and through the mob waiting outside. Reporters shoved microphones in her face. Shouted questions. With one arm shielding her shoulders, Dan shoved through the crowd and down the cement steps to the car that waited for them at the curb, then helped her inside. She was surprised when her uncle got in on the other side. She hadn't even been aware that he'd followed them.

"It could have been worse," her uncle said, trying to reassure. "He could have been convicted of first-degree murder, which would have meant a much longer sentence."

Taryn knew that, but at the moment it was little consolation. Her brother was still going to prison for a long time.

"Here. Drink some of this." Dan shoved a container of bottled water into her hand, and she obediently sipped from it. Throughout the ride, she could barely string her thoughts together. The word *guilty* kept screaming through her head, punctuated by the bangs from the judge's gavel pounding on wood. Once they arrived at her uncle's manor, Taryn hurried upstairs to her room. There, she stretched out on the bed and cried. Physically and emotionally exhausted, she slept.

She was surprised to wake up and see the glow of early morning lighten the window shade. She changed into a clean shirt and slacks then headed downstairs. Only an hour remained until they would leave for the courthouse.

Dan sat at the kitchen table by the recessed bay window, cradling a mug of black coffee. He looked up when she entered.

"I shouldn't have left him like that," Taryn said in greeting. It had been on her mind since she'd woken up. "I deserted him when he needed me most."

"No, you didn't. Before we left for court yesterday, Patrick told me that if he should be found guilty, I was to get you out of there fast." Dan pulled out the wooden chair beside his as an invitation for her to sit down. "Believe me, he understood.

Now grab yourself a plate and let's get some food into you."

Taryn eyed the smorgasbord of scrambled eggs, bagels, mini-sausages, and melon balls that covered the center of the table. Her stomach turned. She hadn't been able to force more than a few spoonfuls of food down yesterday and doubted today would be much different. Yet she needed to eat if she were to endure what would probably be one of the worst days of her life. The day her brother was sent to prison.

"Not now." She looked away from the food and started to rise from the table. "Maybe later. After court."

"Taryn, wait. Before we face the public again, you need to know the worst that could happen." Dan cupped his warm hand over Taryn's cold one, and she sat back down, nodding for him to continue. "I talked to Patrick's lawyer last night. The maximum he could get is eleven years, but since this is Patrick's first time before a judge, that might work in his favor. No one can second-guess a judge, of course, but Mr. Phelps doesn't think Patrick will get more than eight years with probation."

It sounded like an eternity. Taryn closed her eyes and took a deep, shaky breath.

"I have to return to the inn, and I want you to come with me. You need a break from all this. You rarely eat anymore, and you look as if you might blow away."

Taryn nodded, her mind elsewhere.

He squeezed her hand. "It's not your fault. I know what you're thinking. I thought the same thing after Gwen died. That if I'd somehow done something differently or forced her to listen to reason, she might still be alive. But Pastor Trent helped me realize that we're not responsible for others' choices. You heard him that day at church. We can only love and support and pray for those we care about who are doing the wrong thing. What happened to your family is tragic, but maybe it took the circumstances of that shooting for Patrick to make the choice to turn away from drugs and find God. Maybe, unless he ended up at rock bottom, he would've never reached up. We'll just keep praying for Patrick and trust him to God's care during his prison term. I like the guy. Maybe he can even come to Colorado for a visit when he gets out."

Taryn brushed a few tears from her eyes and smiled. "You're beginning to sound as if you could be a minister, like Pastor Trent."

"Scratch that thought!" Dan looked stricken. "Unless God hits me over the head with a two-by-four, that's about the only way I'll consider preaching."

Taryn remembered how well he'd instructed her on the slopes, and how kind, gentle, and encouraging he'd been. "I don't know, I think you would make a great preacher someday."

Dan took a long swig of coffee. He set the mug down and lifted his eyes. "Have you considered what I asked you weeks ago? About becoming my wife?"

Taryn nodded and searched for words. "I know that I love you, Dan. And one day I do want to marry you and become Paul's mother, but I can't think about anything like that right now." She stroked his hand lying on top of hers. "I need time to heal and sort things out. But if it's okay, I'd still like to come with you to Pinecrest. It's so beautiful there; I can't think of any other place I'd like to stay. I can't stay here. Not now. California no longer feels like home, and there might always be publicity each time I set foot outside the house. If not the news reporters, then the paparazzi. Especially since I'll get the full inheritance now."

He lifted her hand to his mouth and kissed the backs of her fingers, staring into her eyes all the while. "I promised I wouldn't rush you into marriage, and I won't. Of course you must come back with me. With Mary's great cooking, Gram's companionship, and Paul's clowning around, we'll have you back to your happy self again in no time."

Taryn considered. "You know, it's funny. But I wonder if I ever was all that happy. It seems like I've been running all my life—either to or from something. When I was a child and a teenager, I ran to seek acceptance but never found it. And after what happened, I ran to your inn because I was afraid. But until I ran into the arms of Jesus—something my mother wrote in one of her letters—I never felt peace. However, since Christmas, in spite of all that's gone on, I've had the strangest calm visit me at times, even when things were at their worst. I can't explain it. I'm starting to feel it now. With you and God supporting me, I think I'll be able to handle anything that comes my way."

Dan stood to his feet, his eyes glistening. "Come here."

Taryn went into his open arms.

He kissed the top of her head and held her tightly. "Your mother was wise. And her daughter has become just as wise."

Taryn smiled against Dan's shirt. "Thank you for being there for me these past weeks. Your strength has helped me so much."

He kissed her then, a tender kiss without expectation but full of promise. Parting, he took her hand, and they left the kitchen to get ready for their last day in court.

epilogue

"When's he gonna be here?" Six-year-old Meagan impatiently peered out the huge picture window, holding her doll at her side so she could see through the frosty glass, too.

That's what Taryn would like to know. She studied the white swirling flakes then forced herself to move away from the outside view.

Settling on a chair, she pulled Patricia close and adjusted the red velvet bow in her dark hair for the fourth time, then threw a warning look to thirteen-year-old Paul, home from school for the holidays and about to pull the green ribbon from four-year-old Becca's hair. The boy, now growing into a man, grinned back and raised his hands in innocence, the loveable quirk of mischief still a part of him. Since he started attending a private school for gifted children three years ago, Taryn had witnessed huge leaps in his emotional growth and a fresh self-confidence.

"Settle down, Taryn," Gram said from her wheelchair by the Christmas tree. "Dan knows these roads better than anybody. He'll be here soon."

Paul, all arms and legs and almost six feet tall, hoisted three-year-old Lindsey high into the air. The girl squealed with delight. "Look, Mommy—I'm fwying!" She snatched a candy cane from the top branches of the tree. "I'm an angel! Can I be an angel?"

Paul chuckled. "It's fun to pretend isn't it, Lindsey?" he said, his voice deeper than Taryn remembered it as he settled the girl against his hip. "But I'd rather you just stay my sister. That's who God made you to be. But anytime you want to pretend, I'll play with you. I used to do a lot of pretending when I was a kid."

Taryn hid a grin. Teenagers.

"Okay." Lindsey licked the top of her candy cane. "Will you read to me, Pauw?"

"Sure. But later, after Dad gets home."

Harry Bowers shuffled behind Paul and slapped him on the back. "Just as long as you don't teach her any of your pranks, young man," he joked, and Paul's face reddened.

Since Harry had married Gram five years ago and joined the family, much of his gruffness disappeared, though he still had his moments. Stranger still, he and Paul had become fast friends, and they often played chess or cards together. Paul always won, but Harry didn't seem to mind.

The crunch of tires rolling over snow made Taryn's heart jump.

"They're here!" Meagan scrambled to the door, trying to turn the bolt.

Taryn was right behind her. "Here, honey, let me." Her hands were trembling, and she almost couldn't work the latch. Impatiently she flung open the door.

Snow flecked the blue stocking cap and padded coat of the man who approached the stoop. His blue-green eyes sparkled.

"Patrick!" she cried and threw her arms around him.

Tears sprang to her eyes as she held her brother at last. Seven long years her twin had been incarcerated, but now he was finally free. Taryn hugged him tightly, letting her emotions soak his coat.

"Shh, Taryn, it's okay," he whispered. "It's all okay now."

"I know," she said and released her death-hold on him. She surveyed his face. "You're thinner than when I visited you last, but you don't look half bad. Actually you look really good." She kissed his bristly cheek.

"I can definitely say the same."

"Are you my uncle Patrick?" Patricia asked shyly.

Patrick hunkered down to his namesake's level. "I sure am. And who might you be?"

She giggled. "I'm Patricia and I'm almost six. Daddy said while you're here you can go with me to ski on the bunny slopes. Wanna come? We go skiing all the time."

"I can ski, too," Meagan threw in.

"Wow, that sounds really neat. Maybe I'll have to give it a try."

"I can teach you," Patricia said, taking Patrick's hand and leading him to the family parlor. "It's lots of fun. We even get to play follow the leader and other games."

Meagan grabbed his other hand. "We already had Christmas, and I got this doll. Isn't she pretty? Mommy says we're going to have another Christmas, though, now that you're here. Even if it is January."

"Are you Mommy's twin?" Becca asked shyly as she moved into the lobby and stopped in front of him. "You don't look alike."

"Boy and girl twins are different," Patrick explained. "You must be Becca. Your mommy said you had hair the color of sweet pumpkin pie—like hers used to be when she was your age."

Becca giggled, her hand over her mouth.

Taryn followed the foursome into the family parlor and watched her little girls flock around Patrick, exhibiting not an ounce of shyness. But that wasn't a surprise since Taryn had been talking about her brother every day for the past few months. Gram and Harry greeted Patrick warmly and smiled. Paul edged close and chuckled when Patrick told a corny joke. Taryn felt Dan's arms slip around her from behind.

"He looks good," Dan whispered near her ear.

"Better than I expected," Taryn agreed, bringing her hand to his arm. She turned her head to kiss the corner of his mouth. "Thank you for braving a snowstorm to collect him at the airport. I was so worried when the weather got bad not ten minutes after you left."

"I was late getting there, but it's a good thing his plane was early. Any later and it might not have been able to land. This looks like some winter storm we're getting."

Taryn leaned her head back against the crook of his shoulder. "Thank God we're all together now, safe and warm."

Basking in her husband's embrace, Taryn watched her family. Patrick was playing Mr. Tickle with Lindsey, who laughed and tried to dodge his wiggling fingers. The other three girls demanded their turn, and Paul took up the game, trying to tickle Becca, Meagan, and Patricia as they each took challenging steps his way, then darted back in retreat. Harry and Gram toasted each other with crystal cups of eggnog, their expressions tender as they gazed at one another.

Hearing the peals of children's laughter, seeing the warm smiles, knowing that God had blessed them so, Taryn felt another emotional wave hit her. She turned in her husband's arms.

"I love you so much, Dan. This is the best Christmas ever. Thank you for making it possible."

He smiled then lowered his mouth to meet hers in a kiss as warm and reassuring as a cozy fire. A place from which she never wanted to run.

Home.

A Letter To Our Readers

Dear Reader:

In order that we might better contribute to your reading enjoyment, we would appreciate your taking a few minutes to respond to the following questions. We welcome your comments and read each form and letter we receive. When completed, please return to the following:

Fiction Editor
Heartsong Presents
PO Box 719
Uhrichsville, Ohio 44683

1. Did you enjoy reading *Run Fast My Love* by Pamela Griffin?
   ❏ Very much! I would like to see more books by this author!
   ❏ Moderately. I would have enjoyed it more if

   _____

   _____

   _____

2. Are you a member of **Heartsong Presents**? ❏ Yes ❏ No
   If no, where did you purchase this book? _____

   _____

3. How would you rate, on a scale from 1 (poor) to 5 (superior),
   the cover design? _____

4. On a scale from 1 (poor) to 10 (superior), please rate the
   following elements.

   ____ Heroine   ____ Plot
   ____ Hero   ____ Inspirational theme
   ____ Setting   ____ Secondary characters

5. These characters were special because?_____

_____

_____

6. How has this book inspired your life?_____

_____

_____

7. What settings would you like to see covered in future
   Heartsong Presents books? _____

_____

_____

8. What are some inspirational themes you would like to see
   treated in future books? _____

_____

_____

9. Would you be interested in reading other **Heartsong
   Presents** titles? ❑ Yes ❑ No

10. Please check your age range:
   ❑ Under 18   ❑ 18-24
   ❑ 25-34   ❑ 35-45
   ❑ 46-55   ❑ Over 55

Name_____

Occupation _____

Address _____

City_____ State_____ Zip_____

Heart♥ong

Any 12 Heartsong Presents titles for only $27.00*

CONTEMPORARY ROMANCE IS CHEAPER BY THE DOZEN!

Buy any assortment of twelve *Heartsong Presents* titles and save 25% off of the already discounted price of $2.97 each!

*plus $2.00 shipping and handling per order and sales tax where applicable.

HEARTSONG PRESENTS TITLES AVAILABLE NOW:

___HP265 *Hearth of Fire*, C. L. Reece
___HP278 *Elizabeth's Choice*, L. Lyle
___HP298 *A Sense of Belonging*, T. Fowler
___HP302 *Seasons*, G. G. Martin
___HP305 *Call of the Mountain*, Y. Lehman
___HP306 *Piano Lessons*, G. Sattler
___HP317 *Love Remembered*, A. Bell
___HP318 *Born for This Love*, B. Bancroft
___HP321 *Fortress of Love*, M. Panagiotopoulos
___HP322 *Country Charm*, D. Mills
___HP325 *Gone Camping*, G. Sattler
___HP326 *A Tender Melody*, B. L. Etchison
___HP329 *Meet My Sister, Tess*, K. Billerbeck
___HP330 *Dreaming of Castles*, G. G. Martin
___HP337 *Ozark Sunrise*, H. Alexander
___HP338 *Somewhere a Rainbow*, Y. Lehman
___HP341 *It Only Takes a Spark*, P. K. Tracy
___HP342 *The Haven of Rest*, A. Boeshaar
___HP349 *Wild Tiger Wind*, G. Buck
___HP350 *Race for the Roses*, L. Snelling
___HP353 *Ice Castle*, J. Livingston
___HP354 *Finding Courtney*, B. L. Etchison
___HP361 *The Name Game*, M. G. Chapman
___HP377 *Come Home to My Heart*, J. A. Grote
___HP378 *The Landlord Takes a Bride*, K. Billerbeck
___HP390 *Love Abounds*, A. Bell
___HP394 *Equestrian Charm*, D. Mills
___HP401 *Castle in the Clouds*, A. Boeshaar
___HP402 *Secret Ballot*, Y. Lehman
___HP405 *The Wife Degree*, A. Ford
___HP406 *Almost Twins*, G. Sattler
___HP409 *A Living Soul*, H. Alexander
___HP410 *The Color of Love*, D. Mills
___HP413 *Remnant of Victory*, J. Odell
___HP414 *The Sea Beckons*, B. L. Etchison
___HP417 *From Russia with Love*, C. Coble
___HP418 *Yesteryear*, G. Brandt
___HP421 *Looking for a Miracle*, W. E. Brunstetter

___HP422 *Condo Mania*, M. G. Chapman
___HP425 *Mustering Courage*, L. A. Coleman
___HP426 *To the Extreme*, T. Davis
___HP429 *Love Ahoy*, C. Coble
___HP430 *Good Things Come*, J. A. Ryan
___HP433 *A Few Flowers*, G. Sattler
___HP434 *Family Circle*, J. L. Barton
___HP438 *Out in the Real World*, K. Paul
___HP441 *Cassidy's Charm*, D. Mills
___HP442 *Vision of Hope*, M. H. Flinkman
___HP445 *McMillian's Matchmakers*, G. Sattler
___HP449 *An Ostrich a Day*, N. J. Farrier
___HP450 *Love in Pursuit*, D. Mills
___HP454 *Grace in Action*, K. Billerbeck
___HP458 *The Candy Cane Calaboose*, J. Spaeth
___HP461 *Pride and Pumpernickel*, A. Ford
___HP462 *Secrets Within*, G. G. Martin
___HP465 *Talking for Two*, W. E. Brunstetter
___HP466 *Risa's Rainbow*, A. Boeshaar
___HP469 *Beacon of Truth*, P. Griffin
___HP470 *Carolina Pride*, T. Fowler
___HP473 *The Wedding's On*, G. Sattler
___HP474 *You Can't Buy Love*, K. Y'Barbo
___HP477 *Extreme Grace*, T. Davis
___HP478 *Plain and Fancy*, W. E. Brunstetter
___HP481 *Unexpected Delivery*, C. M. Hake
___HP482 *Hand Quilted with Love*, J. Livingston
___HP485 *Ring of Hope*, B. L. Etchison
___HP486 *The Hope Chest*, W. E. Brunstetter
___HP489 *Over Her Head*, G. G. Martin
___HP490 *A Class of Her Own*, J. Thompson
___HP493 *Her Home or Her Heart*, K. Elaine
___HP494 *Mended Wheels*, A. Bell & J. Sagal
___HP497 *Flames of Deceit*, R. Dow & A. Snaden
___HP498 *Charade*, P. Humphrey
___HP501 *The Thrill of the Hunt*, T. H. Murray
___HP502 *Whole in One*, A. Ford
___HP505 *Happily Ever After*, M. Panagiotopoulos

(If ordering from this page, please remember to include it with the order form.)

Presents

Great Inspirational Romance at a Great Price!

Heartsong Presents books are inspirational romances in contemporary and historical settings, designed to give you an enjoyable, spirit-lifting reading experience. You can choose wonderfully written titles from some of today's best authors like Hannah Alexander, Andrea Boeshaar, Yvonne Lehman, Tracie Peterson, and many others.

When ordering quantities less than twelve, above titles are $2.97 each.
Not all titles may be available at time of order.